TEXTBOOK EDITION

THE CHRONICLES
OF AMERICA SERIES
ALLEN JOHNSON
EDITOR

GERHARD R. LOMER
CHARLES W. JEFFERYS
ASSISTANT EDITORS

THE DESCENT OF THE FRASER RIVER, 1808
From the painting by C. W. Jefferys

THE
CANADIAN DOMINION

A CHRONICLE OF
OUR NORTHERN NEIGHBOR
BY OSCAR D. SKELTON

NEW HAVEN: YALE UNIVERSITY PRESS
TORONTO: GLASGOW, BROOK & CO.
LONDON: HUMPHREY MILFORD
OXFORD UNIVERSITY PRESS

PREFACE

THE history of Canada since the close of the French régime falls into three clearly marked half centuries. The first fifty years after the Peace of Paris determined that Canada was to maintain a separate existence under the British flag and was not to become a fourteenth colony or be merged with the United States. The second fifty years brought the winning of self-government and the achievement of Confederation. The third fifty years witnessed the expansion of the Dominion from sea to sea and the endeavor to make the unity of the political map a living reality — the endeavor to weld the far-flung provinces into one country, to give Canada a distinctive place in the Empire and in the world, and eventually in the alliance of peoples banded together in mankind's greatest task of enforcing peace and justice among nations.

The author has found it expedient in this narrative to depart from the usual method of these

Chronicles and arrange the matter in chronological rather than in biographical or topical divisions. The first period of fifty years is accordingly covered in one chapter, the second in two chapters, and the third in two chapters. Authorities and a list of publications for a more extended study will be found in the Bibliographical Note.

O. D. S.

QUEEN'S UNIVERSITY,
KINGSTON, CANADA,
July, 1919.

CONTENTS

THE CANADIAN DOMINION

CHAPTER I

THE FIRST FIFTY YEARS

SCARCELY more than half a century has passed since the Dominion of Canada, in its present form, came into existence. But thrice that period has elapsed since the fateful day when Montcalm and Wolfe laid down their lives in battle on the Plains of Abraham, and the lands which now comprise the Dominion finally passed from French hands and came under British rule.

The Peace of Paris, which brought the Seven Years' War to a close in 1763, marked the termination of the empire of France in the New World. Over the continent of North America, after that peace, only two flags floated, the red and yellow banner of Spain and the Union Jack of Great Britain. Of these the Union Jack held sway over

by far the larger domain — over the vague territories about Hudson Bay, over the great valley
of the St. Lawrence, and over all the lands lying
east of the Mississippi, save only New Orleans.
To whom it would fall to develop this vast claim,
what mighty empires would be carved out of the
wilderness, where the boundary lines would run between the nations yet to be, were secrets the future held.   Yet in retrospect it is now clear that in
solving these questions the Peace of Paris played
no inconsiderable part.   By removing from the
American colonies the menace of French aggression from the north it relieved them of a sense of
dependence on the mother country and so made
possible the birth of a new nation in the United
States.   At the same time, in the northern half
of the continent, it made possible that other experiment in democracy, in the union of diverse
races, in international neighborliness, and in the
reconciliation of empire with liberty, which Canada
presents to the whole world, and especially to her
elder sister in freedom.

In 1763 the territories which later were to
make up the Dominion of Canada were divided
roughly into three parts.   These parts had little or
nothing in common.   They shared together neither

traditions of suffering or glory nor ties of blood or trade. Acadia, or Nova Scotia, by the Atlantic, was an old French colony, now British for over a generation. Canada, or Quebec, on the St. Lawrence and the Great Lakes, with seventy thousand French habitants and a few hundred English camp followers, had just passed under the British flag. West and north lay the vaguely outlined domains of the Hudson's Bay Company, where the red man and the buffalo still reigned supreme and almost unchallenged.

The old colony of Acadia, save only the island outliers, Cape Breton and Prince Edward Island, now ceded by the Peace of Paris, had been in British hands since 1713. It was not, however, until 1749 that any concerted effort had been made at a settlement of this region. The menace from the mighty fortress which the French were rebuilding at that time at Louisbourg, in Cape Breton, and the hostility of the restless Acadians or old French settlers on the mainland, had compelled action and the British Government departed from its usual policy of *laissez faire* in matters of emigration. Twenty-five hundred English settlers were brought out to found and hold the town and fort of Halifax. Nearly as many Germans were planted in Lunenburg, where their descendants flourish to this day. Then the hapless Acadians were driven into exile and into the room they left, New Englanders of strictest Puritan ancestry came, on their own initiative, and built up new communities like those of Massachusetts, Connecticut, and Rhode Island. Other waves of voluntary immigration followed — Ulster Presbyterians, driven out by the attempt of England to crush the Irish woolen manufacture, and, still later, Highlanders, Roman Catholic and Presbyterian, who soon made Gaelic the prevailing tongue of the easternmost counties. By 1767 the colony of Nova Scotia, which then included all Acadia, north and east of Maine, had a prosperous population of some seven thousand Americans, two thousand Irish, two thousand Germans, barely a thousand English, and well over a thousand surviving Acadian French. In short, this northernmost of the Atlantic colonies appeared to be fast on the way to become a part of New England. It was chiefly New Englanders who had peopled it, and it was with New England that for many a year its whole social and commercial intercourse was carried on. It was no accident that Nova Scotia later produced the first Yankee humorist, "Sam Slick."

With the future sister province of Canada, or Quebec, which lay along the St. Lawrence as far as the Great Lakes, Acadia or Nova Scotia had much less in common than with New England. Hundreds of miles of unbroken forest wilderness lay between the two colonies, and the sea lanes ran between the St. Lawrence, the Bay of Fundy, or Halifax and Havre or Plymouth, and not between Quebec and Halifax. Even the French settlers came of different stocks. The Acadians were chiefly men of La Rochelle and the Loire, while the Canadians came, for the most part, from the coast provinces stretching from Normandy and Picardy to Poitou and Bordeaux.

The situation in Canada proper presented the British authorities with a problem new in their imperial experience. Hitherto, save for Acadia and New Netherland, where the settlers were few in numbers and, even in New Netherland, closely akin to the conquerors in race, religion, and speech, no colony containing men of European stocks had been acquired by conquest. Canada held some sixty or seventy thousand settlers, French and Catholic almost to a man. Despite the inefficiency of French colonial methods the plantation had taken firm root. The colony had developed a strength, a social structure, and an individuality all its own. Along the St. Lawrence and the Richelieu the settlements lay close and compact; the habitants' whitewashed cottages lined the river banks only a few *arpents* apart. The social cohesion of the colony was equally marked. Alike in government, in religion, and in industry, it was a land where authority was strong. Governor and intendant, feudal seigneur, bishop and Jesuit superior, ruled each in his own sphere and provided a rigid mold and framework for the growth of the colony. There were, it is true, limits to the reach of the arm of authority. Beyond Montreal stretched a vast wilderness merging at some uncertain point into the other wilderness that was Louisiana. Along the waterways which threaded this great No Man's Land the *coureurs-de-bois* roamed with little heed to law or license, glad to escape from the paternal strictness that irked youth on the lower St. Lawrence. But the liberty of these rovers of the forest was not liberty after the English pattern; the *coureur-de-bois* was of an entirely different type from the pioneers of British stock who were even then pushing their way through the gaps in the Alleghanies and making homes in the backwoods. Priest and seigneur, habitant and *coureur-de-bois*, were one and all difficult to fit into accepted English ways. Clearly Canada promised to strain the digestive capacity of the British lion.

The present western provinces of the Dominion were still the haunt of Indian and buffalo. French-Canadian explorers and fur traders, it is true, had penetrated to the Rockies a few years before the Conquest, and had built forts on Lake Winnipeg, on the Assiniboine and Red rivers, and at half a dozen portages on the Saskatchewan. But the "Company of Adventurers of England trading into Hudson's Bay" had not yet ventured inland, still content to carry on its trade with the Indians from its forts along the shores of that great sea. On the Pacific the Russians had coasted as far south as Mount Saint Elias, but no white man, so far as is known, had set foot on the shores of what is now British Columbia.

Two immediate problems were bequeathed to the British Government by the Treaty of Paris: what was to be done with the unsettled lands between the Alleghanies and the Mississippi; and how were the seventy thousand French subjects in the valley of the St. Lawrence to be dealt with? The first difficulty was not solved. It was merely postponed. The whole back country of the English colonies was proclaimed an Indian reserve where the King's white subjects might trade but might not acquire land. This policy was not devised in order to set bounds to the expansion of the older colonies; that was an afterthought. The policy had its root in an honest desire to protect the Indians from the frauds of unscrupulous traders and from the encroachments of settlers on their hunting grounds. The need of a conciliatory, if firm, policy in regard to the great interior was made evident by the Pontiac rising in 1763, the aftermath of the defeat of the French, who had done all they could to inspire the Indians with hatred for the advancing English.

How to deal with Canada was a more thorny problem. The colony had not been sought by its conquerors for itself. It was counted of little worth. The verdict of its late possessors, as recorded in Voltaire's light farewell to "a few arpents of snow," might be discounted as an instance of sour grapes; but the estimate of its new possessors was evidently little higher, since they debated long and dubiously whether in the peace settlement they should retain Canada or the little sugar island of Guadeloupe, a mere pin point on the map. Canada had been conquered not for the good it might bring but for the harm it was doing as a base for French attack upon the English colonies — "the wasps' nest must be smoked out." But once it had been taken, it had to be dealt with for itself.

The policy first adopted was a simple one, natural enough for eighteenth-century Englishmen. They decided to make Canada[1] over in the image of the old colonies, to turn the "new subjects," as they were called, in good time into Englishmen and Protestants. A generation or two would suffice, in the phrase of Francis Masères — himself a descendant of a Huguenot refugee but now wholly an Englishman — for "melting down the French nation into the English in point of language, affections, religion, and laws." Immigration was to be encouraged from Britain and from the other American colonies, which, in the view of the Lords of Trade, were already overstocked and in danger of being forced by the scarcity or monopoly of land to take up manufactures which would

[1] The Royal Proclamation of 1763 set the bounds of the new colony. They were surprisingly narrow, a mere strip along both sides of the St. Lawrence from a short distance beyond the Ottawa on the west, to the end of the Gaspé peninsula on the east. The land to the northeast was put under the jurisdiction of the Governor of Newfoundland, and the Great Lakes region was included in the territory reserved for the Indians.

compete with English wares. And since it would greatly contribute to speedy settlement, so the Royal Proclamation of 1763 declared, that the King's subjects should be informed of his paternal care for the security of their liberties and properties, it was promised that, as soon as circumstances would permit, a General Assembly would be summoned, as in the older colonies. The laws of England, civil and criminal, as near as might be, were to prevail. The Roman Catholic subjects were to be free to profess their own religion, "so far as the laws of Great Britain permit," but they were to be shown a better way. To the first Governor instructions were issued "that all possible Encouragement shall be given to the erecting Protestant Schools in the said Districts, Townships and Precincts, by settling and appointing and allotting proper Quantities of Land for that Purpose and also for a Glebe and Maintenance for a Protestant minister and Protestant schoolmasters." Thus in the fullness of time, like Acadia, but without any Evangeline of Grand Pré, without any drastic policy of expulsion, impossible with seventy thousand people scattered over a wide area, even Canada would become a good English land, a newer New England.

It is questionable whether this policy could ever have achieved success even if it had been followed for generations without rest or turning. But it was not destined to be given a long trial. From the very beginning the men on the spot, the soldier Governors of Canada, urged an entirely contrary policy on the Home Government, and the pressure of events soon brought His Majesty's Ministers to concur.

As the first civil Governor of Canada, the British authorities chose General Murray, one of Wolfe's ablest lieutenants, who since 1760 had served as military Governor of the Quebec district. He was to be aided in his task by a council composed of the Lieutenant Governors of Montreal and Three Rivers, the Chief Justice, the head of the customs, and eight citizens to be named by the Governor from "the most considerable of the persons of property" in the province.

The new Governor was a blunt, soldierly man, upright and just according to his lights, but deeply influenced by his military and aristocratic leanings. Statesmen thousands of miles away might plan to encourage English settlers and English political ways and to put down all that was French. To the man on the spot English settlers meant "the four hundred and fifty contemptible sutlers and traders" who had come in the wake of the army from New England and New York, with no proper respect for their betters, and vulgarly and annoyingly insistent upon what they claimed to be their rights. The French might be alien in speech and creed, but at least the seigneurs and the higher clergy were gentlemen, with a due respect for authority, the King's and their own, and the habitants were docile, the best of soldier stuff. "Little, very little," Murray wrote in 1764 to the Lords of Trade, "will content the New Subjects, but nothing will satisfy the Licentious Fanaticks Trading here, but the expulsion of the Canadians, who are perhaps the bravest and best race upon the Globe, a Race, who cou'd they be indulged with a few priviledges wch the Laws of England deny to Roman Catholicks at home, wou'd soon get the better of every National Antipathy to their Conquerors and become the most faithful and most useful set of Men in this American Empire."[1]

Certainly there was much in the immediate

---

[1] This quotation and those following in this chapter are from official documents most conveniently assembled in Shortt and Doughty, *Documents relating to the Constitutional History of Canada, 1759–1791,* and Doughty and McArthur, *Documents relating to the Constitutional History of Canada, 1791–1818.*

situation to justify Murray's attitude. It was preposterous to set up a legislature in which only the four hundred Protestants might sit and from which the seventy thousand Catholics would be barred. It would have been difficult in any case to change suddenly the system of laws governing the most intimate transactions of everyday life. But when, as happened, the Administration was entrusted in large part to newly created justices of the peace, men with "little French and less honour," "to whom it is only possible to speak with guineas in one's hand," the change became flatly impossible. Such an alteration, if still insisted upon, must come more slowly than the impatient traders in Montreal and Quebec desired.

The British Government, however, was not yet ready to abandon its policy. The Quebec traders petitioned for Murray's recall, alleging that the measures required to encourage settlement had not been adopted, that the Governor was encouraging factions by his partiality to the French, that he treated the traders with "a Rage and Rudeness of Language and Demeanor" and — a fair thrust in return for his reference to them as "the most immoral collection of men I ever knew" — as "discountenancing the Protestant Religion by almost

a Total Neglect of Attendance upon the Service of
the Church." When the London business correspondents of the traders backed up this petition,
the Government gave heed. In 1766 Murray was
recalled to England and, though he was acquitted
of the charges against him, he did not return to
his post in Canada.

The triumph of the English merchants was short.
They had jumped from the frying pan into the
fire. General Guy Carleton, Murray's successor
and brother officer under Wolfe, was an even abler
man, and he was still less in sympathy with democracy of the New England pattern. Moreover, a
new factor had come in to reënforce the soldier's
instinctive preference for gentlemen over shopkeepers. The first rumblings of the American
Revolution had reached Quebec. It was no time,
in Carleton's view, to set up another sucking republic. Rather, he believed, the utmost should
be made of the opportunity Canada afforded as a
barrier against the advance of democracy, a curb
upon colonial insolence. The need of cultivating
the new subjects was the greater, Carleton contended, because the plan of settlement by Englishmen gave no sign of succeeding: "barring a
Catastrophe shocking to think of, this Country

must, to the end of Time, be peopled by the Canadian race."

To bind the Canadians firmly to England, Carleton proposed to work chiefly through their old leaders, the seigneurs and the clergy. He would restore to the people their old system of laws, both civil and criminal. He would confirm the seigneurs in their feudal dues and fines, which the habitants were growing slack in paying now that the old penalties were not enforced, and he would give them honors and emoluments such as they had before enjoyed as officers in regular or militia regiments. The Roman Catholic clergy were already, in fact, confirmed in their right to tithe and toll; and, without objection from the Governor, Bishop Briand, elected by the chapter in Quebec and consecrated in Paris, once more assumed control over the flock.

Carleton's proposals did not pass unquestioned. His own chief legal adviser, Francis Masères, was a sturdy adherent of the older policy, though he agreed that the time was not yet ripe for setting up an Assembly and suggested some well-considered compromise between the old laws and the new. The Advocate General of England, James Marriott, urged the same course. The policy of 1763, he contended eleven years later, had already succeeded in great measure. The assimilation of government had been effected; an assimilation of manners would follow. The excessive military spirit of the inhabitants had begun to dwindle, as England's interest required. The back settlements of New York and Canada were fast being joined. Two or three thousand men of British stock, many of them men of substance, had gone to the new colony; warehouses and foundries were being built; and many of the principal seigneuries had passed into English hands. All that was needed, he concluded, was persistence along the old path. The same view was of course strenuously urged by the English merchants in the colony, who continued to demand, down to the very eve of the Revolution, an elective Assembly and other rights of freeborn Britons.

Carleton carried the day. His advice, tendered at close range during four years' absentee residence in London, from 1770 to 1774, fell in with the mood of Lord North's Government. The measure in which the new policy was embodied, the famous Quebec Act of 1774, was essentially a part of the ministerial programme for strengthening British power to cope with the resistance then rising to rebellious heights in the old colonies. Though not, as was long believed, designed in retaliation for the Boston disturbances, it is clear that its framers had Massachusetts in mind when deciding on their policy for Quebec. The main purpose of the Act, the motive which turned the scale against the old Anglicizing policy, was to attach the leaders of French-Canadian opinion firmly to the British Crown, and thus not only to prevent Canada itself from becoming infected with democratic contagion or turning in a crisis toward France, but to ensure, if the worst came to the worst, a military base in that northland whose terrors had in old days kept the seaboard colonies circumspectly loyal. Ministers in London had been driven by events to accept Carleton's paradox, that to make Quebec British, it must be prevented from becoming English. If in later years the solidarity and aloofness of the French-Canadian people were sometimes to prove inconvenient to British interests, it was always to be remembered that this situation was due in great part to the deliberate action of Great Britain in strengthening French-Canadian institutions as a means of advancing what she considered her own interests in America. "The views of the British Government in respect to the political uses to which it means to make Canada subservient," Marriott had truly declared, "must direct the spirit of any code of laws."

The Quebec Act multiplied the area of the colony sevenfold by the restoration of all Labrador on the east and the region west as far as the Ohio and the Mississippi and north to the Hudson's Bay Company's territory. It restored the old French civil law but continued the milder English criminal law already in operation. It gave to the Roman Catholic inhabitants the free exercise of their religion, subject to a modified oath of allegiance, and confirmed the clergy in their right "to hold, receive and enjoy their accustomed dues and rights, with respect to such persons only as shall confess the said religion." The promised elective Assembly was not granted, but a Council appointed by the Crown received a measure of legislative power.

On his return to Canada in September, 1774, Carleton reported that the Canadians had "testified the strongest marks of Joy and Gratitude and Fidelity to their King and to His Government for the late Arrangements made at Home in their Favor." The "most respectable part of the

ns of those whom he met
eople had been governed
r many years," he now wrote
d imbibed too much of the
icentiousness and Independ-
y a numerous and turbulent
suddenly restored to a proper
dination." A few of the habit-
rces; fewer joined the invaders
plies — till they grew suspicious
entals." But the majority held
Even when France joined the
s and Admiral d'Estaing appealed
s to rise, they did not heed; though
o say what the result would have
ington had agreed to Lafayette's
int French and American invasion

tia also held aloof, in spite of the fact
of the men who had come from New
nd from Ulster were eager to join the
the south. In Nova Scotia democracy
ss hardy plant than in Massachusetts.
n and township institutions, which had
e nurseries of resistance in New England,
t been allowed to take root there. The

English," he continued, urged peaceful acceptance of the new order. Evidently, however, the respectable members of society were few, as the great body of the English settlers joined in a petition for the repeal of the Act on the ground that it deprived them of the incalculable benefits of habeas corpus and trial by jury. The Montreal merchants, whether, as Carleton commented, they "were of a more turbulent Turn, or that they caught the Fire from some Colonists settled among them," were particularly outspoken in the town meetings they held. In the older colonies the opposition was still more emphatic. An Act which hemmed them in to the seacoast, established on the American continent a Church they feared and hated, and continued an autocratic political system, appeared to many to be the undoing of the work of Pitt and Wolfe and the revival on the banks of the St. Lawrence and the Mississippi of a serious menace to their liberty and progress.

Then came the clash at Lexington, and the War of American Independence had begun. The causes, the course, and the ending of that great civil war have been treated elsewhere in this series.[1] Here

[1] See *The Eve of the Revolution* and *Washington and His Comrades in Arms* (in *The Chronicles of America*).

it is necessary only to note its bearings on the fate of Canada.

Early in 1775 the Continental Congress undertook the conquest of Canada, or, as it was more diplomatically phrased, the relief of its inhabitants from British tyranny. Richard Montgomery led an expedition over the old route by Lake Champlain and the Richelieu, along which French and Indian raiding parties used to pass years before, and Benedict Arnold made a daring and difficult march up the Kennebec and down the Chaudière to Quebec. Montreal fell to Montgomery; and Carleton himself escaped capture only by the audacity of some French-Canadian *voyageurs*, who, under cover of darkness, rowed his whaleboat or paddled it with their hands silently past the American sentinels on the shore. Once down the river and in Quebec, Carleton threw himself with vigor and skill into the defense of his capital. His generalship and the natural strength of the position proved more than a match for Montgomery and Arnold. Montgomery was killed and Arnold wounded in a vain attempt to carry the city by storm on the last night of 1775. At Montreal a delegation from Congress, composed of Benjamin Franklin, Samuel Chase, and Charles Carroll of

circumstances of the founding of Halifax had given rise to a greater tendency, which lasted long, to lean upon the mother country. The Maine wilderness made intercourse between Nova Scotia and New England difficult by land, and the British fleet was in control of the sea until near the close of the war. Nova Scotia stood by Great Britain, and was reserved to become part of a northern nation still in the making.

That nation was to owe its separate existence to the success of the American Revolution. But for that event, coming when it did, the struggling colonies of Quebec and Nova Scotia would in time have become merged with the colonies to the south and would have followed them, whether they remained within the British Empire or not. Thus it was due to the quarrel between the thirteen colonies and the motherland that Canada did not become merely a fourteenth colony or state. Nor was this the only bearing of the Revolution on Canada's destiny. Thanks to the coming of the Loyalists, those exiles of the Revolution who settled in Canada in large numbers, Canada was after all to be dominantly a land of English speech and of English sympathies. By one of the many paradoxes which mark the history of Canada, the very success of the plan which aimed to save British power by confirming French-Canadian nationality and the loyalty of the French led in the end to making a large part of Canada English. The Revolution meant also that for many a year those in authority in England and in Canada itself were to stand in fear of the principles and institutions which had led the old colonies to rebellion and separation, and were to try to build up in Canada buttresses against the advance of democracy.

The British statesmen who helped to frame the Peace of 1783 were men with broad and generous views as to the future of the seceding colonies and their relations with the mother country. It was perhaps inevitable that they should have given less thought to the future of the colonies in America which remained under the British flag. Few men could realize at the moment that out of these scattered fragments a new nation and a second empire would arise. Not only were the seceding colonies given a share in the fishing grounds of Newfoundland and Nova Scotia, which was unfortunately to prove a constant source of friction, but the boundary line was drawn with no thought of the need of broad and easy communication between Nova Scotia and Canada, much less between Canada and the far West. Vague definitions of the boundaries, naturally incident to the prevailing lack of geographical knowledge of the vast continent, held further seeds of trouble. These contentions, however, were far in the future. At the moment another defect of the treaty proved to be Canada's gain. The failure of Lord Shelburne's Ministry to insist upon effective safeguards for the fair treatment of those who had taken the King's side in the old colonies, condemned as it was not only by North and the Tories but by Fox and Sheridan and Burke, led to that Loyalist migration which changed the racial complexion of Canada.

The Treaty of 1783 provided that Congress would "earnestly recommend" to the various States that the Loyalists be granted amnesty and restitution. This pious resolution proved not . worth the paper on which it was written. In State after State the property of the Loyalists was withheld or confiscated anew. Yet this ungenerous treatment of the defeated by the victors is not hard to understand. The struggle had been waged with all the bitterness of civil war. The smallness of the field of combat had intensified personal ill-will.

Both sides had practiced cruelties in guerrilla warfare; but the Patriots forgot Marion's raids, Simsbury mines, and the drumhead hangings, and remembered only Hessian brutalities, Indian scalpings, Tarleton's harryings, and the infamous prison ships of New York. The war had been a long one. The tide of battle had ebbed and flowed. A district that was Patriot one year was frequently Loyalist the next. These circumstances engendered fear and suspicion and led to nervous reprisals.

At least a third, if not a half, of the people of the old colonies had been opposed to revolution. New York was strongly Loyalist, with Pennsylvania, Georgia, and the Carolinas closely following. In the end some fifty or sixty thousand Loyalists abandoned their homes or suffered expulsion rather than submit to the new order. They counted in their ranks many of the men who had held first place in their old communities, men of wealth, of education, and of standing, as well as thousands who had nothing to give but their fidelity to the old order. Many, especially of the well-to-do, went to England; a few found refuge in the West Indies; but the great majority, over fifty thousand in all, sought new homes in the northern wilderness. Over thirty thousand, including many of the most influential of the whole number (with about three thousand negro slaves, afterwards freed and deported to Sierra Leone) were carried by ship to Nova Scotia. They found homes chiefly in that part of the province which in 1784 became New Brunswick. Others, trekking overland or sailing around by the Gulf and up the River, settled in the upper valley of the St. Lawrence — on Lake St. Francis, on the Cataraqui and the Bay of Quinté, and in the Niagara District.

Though these pioneers were generously aided by the British Government with grants of land and supplies, their hardships and disappointments during the first years in the wilderness were such as would have daunted any but brave and desperate men and women whom fate had winnowed. Yet all but a few, who drifted back to their old homes, held out; and the foundations of two more provinces of the future Dominion — New Brunswick and Upper Canada — were thus broadly and soundly laid by the men whom future generations honored as "United Empire Loyalists." Through all the later years, their sacrifices and sufferings, their ideals and prejudices, were to make a deep impress on the development of the nation which they helped to found and were to influence its

relations with the country which they had left
and with the mother country which had held
their allegiance.

Once the first tasks of hewing and hauling and
planting were done, the new settlers called for the
organization of local governments. They were
quite as determined as their late foes to have a
voice in their own governing, even though they
yielded ultimate obedience to rulers overseas.

In the provinces by the sea a measure of self-
government was at once established. New Brunswick received, without question, a constitution on
the Nova Scotia model, with a Lieutenant Governor, an Executive Council appointed to advise him,
which served also as the upper house of the legislature, and an elective Assembly. Of the twenty-
six members of the first Assembly, twenty-three
were Loyalists. With a population so much at
one, and with the tasks of road making and
school building and tax collecting insistent and
absorbing, no party strife divided the province
for many years. In Nova Scotia, too, the Loyalists were in the majority. There, however, the
earlier settlers soon joined with some of the newcomers to form an opposition. The island of

St. John, renamed Prince Edward Island in 1798, had been made a separate Government and had received an Assembly in 1773. Its one absorbing question was the tenure of land. On a single day in 1767 the British authorities had granted the whole island by lottery to army and navy officers and country gentlemen, on condition of the payment of small quitrents. The quitrents were rarely paid, and the tenants of the absentee landlords kept up an agitation for reform which was unceasing but which was not to be successful for a hundred years. In all three Maritime Provinces political and party controversy was little known for a generation after the Revolution.

It was more difficult to decide what form of government should be set up in Canada, now that tens of thousands of English-speaking settlers dwelt beside the old Canadians. Carleton, now Lord Dorchester, had returned as Governor in 1786, after eight years' absence. He was still averse to granting an Assembly so long as the French subjects were in the majority: they did not want it, he insisted, and could not use it. But the Loyalist settlers, not to be put off, joined with the English merchants of Montreal and Quebec in demanding an Assembly and relief from the old French laws. Carleton himself was compelled to admit the force of the conclusion of William Grenville, Secretary of State for the Home Department, then in control of the remnants of the colonial empire, and son of that George Grenville who, as Prime Minister, had introduced the American Stamp Act of 1765: "I am persuaded that it is a point of true Policy to make these Concessions at a time when they may be received as a matter of favour, and when it is in Our own power to regulate and direct the manner of applying them, rather than to wait till they shall be extorted from us by a necessity which shall neither leave us any discretion in the form nor any merit in the substance of what We give." Accordingly, in 1791, the British Parliament passed the Constitutional Act dividing Canada into two provinces separated by the Ottawa River, Lower or French-speaking Canada and Upper or English-speaking Canada, and granting each an elective Assembly.

Thus far the tide of democracy had risen, but thus far only. Few in high places had learned the full lesson of the American Revolution. The majority believed that the old colonies had been lost because they had not been kept under a sufficiently tight rein; that democracy had been allowed too great headway; that the remaining colonies, therefore, should be brought under stricter administrative control; and that care should be taken to build up forces to counteract the democracy which grew so rank and swift in frontier soil. This conservative tendency was strengthened by the outbreak of the French Revolution in 1789.[1] The rulers of England had witnessed two revolutions, and the lesson they drew from both was that it was best to smother democracy in the cradle.

For this reason the measure of representative government that had been granted each of the remaining British colonies in North America was carefully hedged about. The whole executive power remained in the hands of the Governor or his nominees. No one yet conceived it possible that the Assembly should control the Executive Council. The elective Assembly was compelled to share even the law-making power with an upper house, the Legislative Council. Not only were the members of this upper house appointed by the Crown for life, but the King was empowered to bestow hereditary titles upon them with a view

[1] It will be remembered that in the debate on the Constitutional Act the conflicting views of Burke and Fox on the French Revolution led to the dramatic break in their lifelong friendship.

to making the Council in the fullness of time a copy of the House of Lords. A blow was struck even at that traditional prerogative of the popular house, the control of the purse. Carleton had urged that in every township a sixth of the land should be reserved to enable His Majesty "to reward such of His provincial Servants as may merit the Royal favour" and "to create and strengthen an Aristocracy, of which the best use may be made on this Continent, where all Governments are feeble and the general condition of things tends to a wild Democracy." Grenville saw further possibilities in this suggestion. It would give the Crown a revenue which would make it independent of the Assembly, "a measure, which, if it had been adopted when the Old Colonies were first settled, would have retained them to this hour in obedience and Loyalty." Nor was this all. From the same source an endowment might be obtained for a state church which would be a bulwark of order and conservatism. The Constitutional Act accordingly provided for setting aside lands equal in value to one-seventh of all lands granted from time to time, for the support of a Protestant clergy. The Executive Council received power to set up rectories in every parish, to endow them liberally, and to name as rectors ministers of the Church of England. Further, the Executive Council was instructed to retain an equal amount of land as crown reserves, distributed judiciously in blocks between the grants made to settlers. Were any radical tendencies to survive these attentions, the veto power of the British Government could be counted on in the last resort.

For a time the instalment of self-government thus granted satisfied the people. The pioneer years left little leisure for political discussion, nor were there at first any general issues about which men might differ. The Government was carrying on acceptably the essential tasks of surveying, land granting, and road building; and each member of the Assembly played his own hand and was chiefly concerned in obtaining for his constituents the roads and bridges they needed so badly. The English-speaking settlers of Upper Canada were too widely scattered, and the French-speaking citizens of Lower Canada were too ignorant of representative institutions, to act in groups or parties.

Much turned in these early years upon the personality of the Governor. In several instances,

the choice of rulers for the new provinces proved
fortunate. This was particularly so in the case
of John Graves Simcoe, Lieutenant Governor of
Upper Canada from 1792 to 1799. He was a good
soldier and a just and vigorous administrator,
particularly wise in setting his regulars to work
building roads such as Yonge Street and Dundas
Street, which to this day are great provincial
arteries of travel. Yet there were many sources of
weakness in the scheme of government — divided
authority, absenteeism, personal unfitness. When
Dorchester was reappointed in 1786, he had been
made Governor in Chief of all British North America. From the beginning, however, the Lieutenant
Governors of the various provinces asserted independent authority, and in a few years the Governor
General became in fact merely the Governor of
the most populous province, Lower Canada, in
which he resided.

In Upper Canada, as in New Brunswick, the population was at first much at one. In time, however, discordant elements appeared. Religious,
or at least denominational, differences began to
cause friction. The great majority of the early
settlers in Upper Canada belonged to the Church
of England, whose adherents in the older colonies

had nearly all taken the Loyalist side. Of the
Ulster Presbyterians and New England Congrega-
tionalists who formed the backbone of the Revolution, few came to Canada. The growth of the
Methodists and Baptists in the United States
after the Revolution, however, made its mark on
the neighboring country. The first Methodist
class meetings in Upper Canada, held in the United
Empire Loyalist settlement on the Bay of Quinté
in 1791, were organized by itinerant preachers
from the United States; and in the western part
of the province pioneer Baptist evangelists from
the same country reached the scattered settlers
neglected by the older churches.

Nor was it in religion alone that diversity grew.
Simcoe had set up a generous land policy which
brought in many "late Loyalists," American settlers whose devotion to monarchical principles
would not always bear close inquiry. The fan-
tastic experiment of planting in the heart of the
woods of Upper Canada a group of French nobles
driven out by the Revolution left no trace; but
Mennonites, Quakers, and Scottish Highlanders
contributed diverse and permanent factors to the
life of the province. Colonel Thomas Talbot
of Malahide, "a fierce little Irishman who hated

Scotchmen and women, turned teetotallers out of his house, and built the only good road in the province," made the beginnings of settlement midway on Lake Erie. A shrewd Massachusetts merchant, Philemon Wright, with his comrades, their families, servants, horses, oxen, and £10,000, sledged from Boston to Montreal in the winter of 1800, and thence a hundred miles beyond, to found the town of Hull and establish a great lumbering industry in the Ottawa Valley.

These differences of origin and ways of thought had not yet been reflected in political life. Party strife in Upper Canada began with a factional fight which took place in 1805–07 between a group of Irish officeholders and a Scotch clique who held the reins of government. Weekes, an Irish-American barrister, Thorpe, a puisne judge, Wyatt, the surveyor general, and Willcocks, a United Irishman who had become sheriff of one of the four Upper Canada districts, began to question the right to rule of "the Scotch pedlars" or "the Shopkeeper Aristocracy," as Thorpe called those merchants who, for the lack of other leaders, had developed an influence with the governors or ruled in their frequent absence. But the insurgents were backed by only a small minority in the

Assembly, and when the four leaders disappeared from the stage,[1] this curtain raiser to the serious political drama which was to follow came quickly to its end.

In Lower Canada the clash was more serious. The French Canadians, who had not asked for representative government, eventually grasped its possibilities and found leaders other than those ordained for them. In the first Assembly there were many seigneurs and aristocrats who bore names notable for six generations back — Taschereau, Duchesnay, Lotbinière, Rouville, Salaberry. But they soon found their surroundings uncongenial or failed to be reëlected. Writing in 1810 to Lord Liverpool, Secretary of State for War and the Colonies, the Governor, Sir James Craig, with a fine patrician scorn thus pictures the Assembly of his day:

It really, my Lord, appears to me an absurdity, that the Interests of certainly not an unimportant Colony, involving in them those also of no inconsiderable portion of the Commercial concerns of the British Empire,

---

[1] Weekes was slain in a duel. Wyatt and Thorpe were suspended by the Lieutenant Governor, Sir Francis Gore, only to win redress later in England. Willcocks was dismissed from office and fell fighting on the American side in the War of 1812.

should be in the hands of six petty shopkeepers, a
Blacksmith, a Miller, and 15 ignorant peasants who
form part of our present House; a Doctor or Apothe-
cary, twelve Canadian Avocats and Notaries, and four
so far respectable people that at least they do not keep
shops, together with ten English members compleat
the List: there is not one person coming under the
description of a Canadian Gentleman among them.

And again:

A Governor cannot obtain among them even that
sort of influence that might arise from personal intercourse. I can have none with Blacksmiths, Millers,
and Shopkeepers; even the Avocats and Notaries who
compose so considerable a portion of the House, are,
generally speaking, such as I can nowhere meet, except
during the actual sitting of Parliament, when I have
a day of the week expressly appropriated to the receiving
a large portion of them at dinner.

Leadership under these conditions fell to the "un-
principled Demagogues," half-educated lawyers,
men "with nothing to lose."

But it was not merely as an aristocrat facing
peasants and shopkeepers, nor as a soldier faced
by talkers, but as an Englishman on guard against
Frenchmen that Craig found himself at odds with
his Assembly. For nearly twenty years in this
period England was at death grips with France,

and to hate and despise all Frenchmen was part of the hereditary and congenial duty of all true Britons. Craig and those who counseled him were firmly convinced that the new subjects were French at heart. Of the 250,000 inhabitants of Lower Canada, he declared, "about 20,000 or 25,000 may be English or Americans, the rest are French. I use the term designedly, my Lord, because I mean to say that they are in Language, in religion, in manner and in attachment completely French." That there was still some affection for old France, stirred by war and French victories, there is no question, but that the Canadians wished to return to French allegiance was untrue, even though Craig reported that such was "the general opinion of all ranks with whom it is possible to converse on the subject." The French Revolution had created a great gulf between Old France and New France. The clergy did their utmost to bar all intercourse with the land where deism and revolution held sway, and when the Roman Catholic Church and the British Government combined for years on a single object, it was little wonder they succeeded. Nelson's victory at Trafalgar was celebrated by a *Te Deum* in the Roman Catholic Cathedral at Quebec. In fact, as Craig

elsewhere noted, the habitants were becoming
rather a new and distinct nationality, a *nation
canadienne*. They ceased to be French; they declined to become English; and sheltered under their
"Sacred Charter"[1] they became Canadians first
and last.

The governors were not alone in this hostility
to the mass of the people. There had grown up
in the colony a little clique of officeholders, of
whom Jonathan Sewell, the Loyalist Attorney
General, and later Chief Justice, was the chief, full
of racial and class prejudice, and in some cases
greedy for personal gain. Sewell declared it "in-
dispensably necessary to overwhelm and sink the
Canadian population by English Protestants,"
and was even ready to run the risk of bringing in
Americans to effect this end. Of the non-official
English, some were strongly opposed to the pretensions of the "Château Clique"; but others,
and especially the merchants, with their organ the
Quebec *Mercury*, were loud in their denunciations
of the French who were unprogressive and who as

[1] "It cannot be sufficiently inculcated *on the part of Government*
that the Quebec Act is a Sacred Charter, granted by the King in
Parliament to the Canadians as a Security for their Religion, Laws,
and Property." Governor Sir Frederick Haldimand to Lord George
Germaine. Oct. 25, 1780.

landowners were incidentally trying to throw the burden of taxation chiefly on the traders.

The first open sign of the racial division which was to bedevil the life of the province came in 1806 when, in order to meet the attacks of the Anglicizing party, the newspaper *Le Canadien* was established at Quebec. Its motto was significant: "*Notre langue, nos institutions, et nos lois.*" Craig and his counselors took up the challenge. In 1808 he dismissed five militia officers, because of their connection with the irritating journal, and in 1810 he went so far as to suppress it and to throw into prison four of those responsible for its management. The Assembly, which was proving hard to control, was twice dissolved in three years. Naturally the Governor's arbitrary course only stiffened resistance; and passions were rising fast and high when illness led to his recall and the shadow of a common danger from the south, the imminence of war with the United States, for a time drew all men together.

While the foundations of the eastern provinces of Canada were being laid, the wildernesses which one day were to become the western provinces were just rising above the horizon of discovery

In the plains and prairies between the Great Lakes and the Rockies, fur traders warred for the privilege of exchanging with the Indians bad whiskey for good furs. Scottish traders from Montreal, following in the footsteps of La Vérendrye and Niverville, pushed far into the northern wilds.[1] In 1783 the leading traders joined forces in organizing the North-West Company. Their great canoes, manned by French-Canadian *voyageurs*, penetrated the network of waters from the Ottawa to the Saskatchewan, and poured wealth into the pockets of the lordly partners in Montreal. Their rivalry wakened the sleepy Hudson's Bay Company, which was now forced to leave the shores of the inland sea and build posts in the interior.

On the Pacific coast rivalry was still keener. The sea otter and the seal were a lure to the men of many nations. Canada took its part in this rivalry. In 1792, when the Russians were pressing down from their Alaskan posts, when the Spaniards, claiming the Pacific for their own, were exploring the mouth of the Fraser, when

---

[1] It is interesting to note the dominant share taken in the trade and exploration of the North and West by men of Highland Scotch and French extraction. For an account of La Vérendrye see *The Conquest of New France* and for the Scotch fur traders of Montreal see *Adventurers of Oregon* (in *The Chronicles of America*).

Captain Robert Gray of Boston was sailing up the mighty Columbia, and Captain Vancouver was charting the northern coasts for the British Government, a young North-West Company factor, Alexander Mackenzie, in his lonely post on Lake Athabaska, was planning to cross the wilderness of mountains to the coast. With a fellow trader, Mackay, and six Canadian *voyageurs*, he pushed up the Peace and the Parsnip, passed by way of the Fraser and the Blackwater to the Bella Coola, and thence to the Pacific, the first white man to cross the northern continent. Paddling for life through swirling rapids on rivers which rushed madly through sheer rock-bound canyons, swimming for shore when rock or sand bar had wrecked the precious bark canoe, struggling over heartbreaking portages, clinging to the sides of precipices, contending against hostile Indians and fear-stricken followers, and at last winning through, Mackenzie summed up what will ever remain one of the great achievements of exploration in the simple record, painted in vermilion on a rock in Burke Channel: *Alexander Mackenzie, from Canada, by land, the twenty-second of July, one thousand seven hundred and ninety-three.* The first bond had been woven in the union of East and West.

Between the eastern provinces a stronger link was soon to be forged. The War of 1812 gave the scattered British colonies in America for the first time a living sense of unity that transcended all differences, a memory of perils and of victories which nourished a common patriotism.

The War of 1812 was no quarrel of Canada's. It was merely an incident in the struggle between England and Napoleon. At desperate grips, both contestants used whatever weapons lay ready to their hands. Sea power was England's weapon, and in her claim to forbid all neutral traffic with her enemies and to exercise the galling right of search, she pressed it far. France trampled still more ruthlessly on American and neutral rights; but, with memories of 1776 still fresh, the dominant party in the United States was disposed to forgive France and to hold England to strict account.

England had struck at France, regardless of how the blow might injure neutrals. Now the United States sought to strike at England through the colonies, regardless of their lack of any responsibility for English policy. The "war hawks" of the South and West called loudly for the speedy invasion and capture of Canada as a means of punishing England. In so far as the British

North American colonies were but possessions of Great Britain, overseas plantations, the course of the United States could be justified. But potentially these colonies were more than mere possessions. They were a nation in the making, with a right to their own development; they were not simply a pawn in the game of Britain and the United States. Quite aside from the original rights or wrongs of the war, the invasion of Canada was from this standpoint an act of aggression. "Agrarian cupidity, not maritime right, wages this war," insisted John Randolph of Roanoke, the chief opponent of the "war hawks" in Congress. "Ever since the report of the Committee on Foreign Relations came into the House, we have heard but one word — like the whippoorwill, but one eternal monotonous tone — Canada, Canada, Canada!"

At the outset there appeared no question that the conquest of Canada could be, as Jefferson forecast, other than "a mere matter of marching." Eustis, the Secretary of War, prophesied that "we can take Canada without soldiers." Clay insisted that the Canadas were "as much under our command as the Ocean is under Great Britain's." The provinces had barely half a million people, two-thirds of them allied by ties of blood to Britain's chief enemy, to set against the eight millions of the Republic. There were fewer than ten thousand regular troops in all the colonies, half of them down by the sea, far away from the danger zone, and less than fifteen hundred west of Montreal. Little help could come from England, herself at war with Napoleon, the master of half of Europe.

But there was another side. The United States was not a unit in the war; New England was apathetic or hostile to the war throughout, and as late as 1814 two-thirds of the army of Canada were eating beef supplied by Vermont and New York contractors. Weak as was the militia of the Canadas, it was stiffened by English and Canadian regulars, hardened by frontier experience, and led for the most part by trained and able men, whereas an inefficient system and political interference greatly weakened the military force of the fighting States. Above all, the Canadians were fighting for their homes. To them the war was a matter of life and death; to the United States it was at best a struggle to assert commercial rights or national prestige.

The course and fortunes of the war call for only the briefest notice. In the first year the American plans for invading Upper Canada came to grief

through the surrender of Hull at Detroit to Isaac
Brock and the defeat at Queenston Heights of the
American army under Van Rensselaer. The campaign ended with not a foot of Canadian soil in the
invaders' hands, and with Michigan lost, but Brock,
Canada's brilliant leader, had fallen at Queenston,
and at sea the British had tasted unwonted defeat.
In single actions one American frigate after another
proved too much for its British opponent. It was
a rude shock to the Mistress of the Seas.

The second year's campaign was more checkered.
In the West the Americans gained the command of
the Great Lakes by rapid building and good sailing,
and with it followed the command of all the western
peninsula of Upper Canada. The British General Procter was disastrously defeated at Moravian-
town, and his ally, the Shawanoe chief Tecumseh,
one of the half dozen great men of his race, was
killed. York, later known as Toronto, the capital
of the province, was captured, and its public buildings were burned and looted. But in the East fortune was kinder to the Canadians. The American
plan of invasion called for an attack on Montreal from two directions; General Wilkinson was
to sail and march down the St. Lawrence from
Sackett's Harbor with some eight thousand men,

while General Hampton, with four thousand, was to take the historic route by Lake Champlain. Half-way down the St. Lawrence Wilkinson came to grief. Eighteen hundred men whom he landed to drive off a force of a thousand hampering his rear were decisively defeated at Chrystler's Farm. Wilkinson pushed on for a few days, but when word came that Hampton had also met disaster he withdrew into winter quarters. Hampton had found Colonel de Salaberry, with less than sixteen hundred troops, nearly all French Canadians, making a stand on the banks of the Chateauguay, thirty-five miles south of Montreal. He divided his force in order to take the Canadians in front and rear, only to be outmaneuvered and outfought in one of the most brilliant actions of the war and forced to retire. In the closing months of the year the Americans, compelled to withdraw from Fort George on the Niagara, burned the adjoining town of Newark and turned its women and children into the December snow. Drummond, who had succeeded Brock, gained control of both sides of the Niagara and retaliated in kind by laying waste the frontier villages from Lewiston to Buffalo. The year closed with Amherstburg on the Detroit the only Canadian post in American hands.

On the sea the capture of the *Chesapeake* by the *Shannon* salved the pride of England.

The last year of the war was also a year of varying fortunes. In the far West a small body of Canadians and Indians captured Prairie du Chien, on the Mississippi, while Michilimackinac, which a force chiefly composed of French-Canadian *voyageurs* and Indians had captured in the first months of war, defied a strong assault. In Upper Canada the Americans raided the western peninsula from Detroit but made their chief attack on the Niagara frontier. Though they scored no permanent success, they fought well and with a fair measure of fortune. The generals with whom they had been encumbered at the outset of the war, Revolutionary relics or political favorites, had now nearly all been replaced by abler men — Scott, Brown, Izard — and their troops were better trained and better equipped. In July the British forces on the Niagara were decisively beaten at Chippawa. Three weeks later was fought the bloodiest battle on Canadian soil, at Lundy's Lane, either side's victory at the moment but soon followed by the retirement of the invading force. The British had now outbuilt their opponents on Lake Ontario; and, though American ships controlled Lake Erie to the end, the Ontario flotilla aided Drummond, Brock's able successor, in forcing the withdrawal of Izard's forces from the whole peninsula in November. Farther east a third attempt to capture Montreal had been defeated in the spring, after Wilkinson with four thousand men had failed to drive five hundred regulars and militia from the stone walls of Lacolle's Mill.

Until this closing year Britain had been unable, in face of the more vital danger from Napoleon, to send any but trifling reënforcements to what she considered a minor theater of the war. Now, with Napoleon in Elba, she was free to take more vigorous action. Her navy had already swept the daring little fleet of American frigates and American merchant marine from the seas. Now it maintained a close blockade of all the coast and, with troops from Halifax, captured and held the Maine coast north of the Penobscot. Large forces of Wellington's hardy veterans crossed the ocean, sixteen thousand to Canada, four thousand to aid in harrying the Atlantic coast, and later nine thousand to seize the mouth of the Mississippi. Yet, strangely, these hosts fared worse, because of hard fortune and poor leadership, than the handful of militia and regulars who had borne the brunt

of the war in the first two years. Under Ross
they captured Washington and burned the official
buildings; but under Prevost they failed at Platts-
burg; and under Pakenham, in January, 1815, they
failed against Andrew Jackson's sharpshooters at
New Orleans.

Before the last-named fight occurred, peace had
been made. Both sides were weary of the war,
which had now, by the seeming end of the struggle
between England and Napoleon in which it was an
incident, lost whatever it formerly had of reason.
Though Napoleon was still in Elba, Europe was far
from being at rest, and the British Ministers, backed
by Wellington's advice, were keen to end the war.
They showed their contempt for the issues at stake
by sending to the peace conference at Ghent three
commissioners as incompetent as ever represented
a great power, Gambier, Goulburn, and Adams.
To face these the United States had sent John
Quincy Adams, Albert Gallatin, Henry Clay,
James Bayard, and Jonathan Russell, as able and
astute a group of players for great stakes as ever
gathered round a table. In these circumstances
the British representatives were lucky to secure
peace on the basis of the *status quo ante*. Canada
had hoped that sufficient of the unsettled Maine

wilderness would be retained to link up New Brunswick with the inland colony of Quebec, but this proposal was soon abandoned. In the treaty not one of the ostensible causes of the war was even mentioned.

The war had the effect of unifying Canadian feeling. Once more it had been determined that Canada was not to lose her identity in the nation to the south. In Upper Canada, especially in the west, there were many recent American settlers who sympathized openly with their kinsmen, but of these some departed, some were jailed, and others had a change of heart. Lower Canada was a unit against the invader, and French-Canadian troops on every occasion covered themselves with glory. To the Canadians, as the smaller people, and as the people whose country had been the chief battle ground, the war in later years naturally bulked larger than to their neighbors. It left behind it unfortunate legacies of hostility to the United States and, among the governing classes, of deep-rooted opposition to its democratic institutions. But it left also memories precious for a young people — the memory of Brock and Macdonell and De Salaberry, of Laura Secord and her daring tramp through the woods to warn of

American attacks, of Stony Creek and Lundy's Lane, Chrystler's Farm and Chateauguay, the memory of sacrifice, of endurance, and of courage that did not count the odds.

Nor were the evil legacies to last for all time. Three years after peace had been made the statesmen of the United States and of Great Britain had the uncommon sense to take a great step toward banishing war between the neighbor peoples. The Rush-Bagot Convention, limiting the naval armament on the Great Lakes to three vessels not exceeding one hundred tons each, and armed only with one eighteen-pounder, though not always observed in the letter, proved the beginning of a sane relationship which has lasted for a century. Had not this agreement nipped naval rivalry in the bud, fleets and forts might have lined the shores and increased the strain of policy and the likelihood of conflict. The New World was already preparing to sound its message to the Old.

CHAPTER II

THE FIGHT FOR SELF-GOVERNMENT

THE history of British North America in the quarter of a century that followed the War of 1812 is in the main the homely tale of pioneer life. Slowly little clearings in the vast forest were widened and won to order and abundance; slowly community was linked to community; and out of the growing intercourse there developed the complex of ways and habits and interests that make up the everyday life of a people.

All the provinces called for settlers, and they did not call in vain. For a time northern New England continued to overflow into the Eastern Townships of Lower Canada, the rolling lands south of the St. Lawrence which had been left untouched by river-bound seigneur and habitant. Into Upper Canada, as well, many individual immigrants came from the south, some of the best the Republic had to give, merchants and manufacturers with little capital but much shrewd enterprise, but also some it could best spare, fugitives from justice and keepers of the taverns that adorned every four corners. Yet slowly this inflow slackened. After the war the Canadian authorities sought to avoid republican contagion and moreover the West of the United States itself was calling for men.

But if fewer came in across the border, many more sailed from across the seas. Not again until the twentieth century were the northern provinces to receive so large a share of British emigrants as came across in the twenties and thirties. Swarms were preparing to leave the overcrowded British hives. Corn laws and poor laws and famine, power-driven looms that starved the cottage weaver, peace that threw an army on a crowded and callous labor market, landlords who rack-rented the Connaught-man's last potato or cleared Highland glens of folks to make way for sheep, rulers who persisted in denying the masses any voice in their own government — all these combined to drive men forth in tens of thousands. Australia was still a land of convict settlements and did not attract free men. To most the United States was the land of promise. Yet, thanks to state aid, private philanthropy, landlords' urging and cheap fares on the ships that came to St. John and Quebec for timber, Canada and the provinces by the sea received a notable share. In the quarter of a century following the peace with Napoleon, British North America received more British emigrants than the United States and the Australian colonies together, though many were merely birds of passage.

The country west of the Great Lakes did not share in this flood of settlement, except for one tragic interlude. Lord Selkirk, a Scotchman of large sympathy and vision, convinced that emigration was the cure for the hopeless misery he saw around him, acquired a controlling interest in the Hudson's Bay Company, and sought to plant colonies in a vast estate granted from its domains. Between 1811 and 1815 he sent out to Hudson Bay, and thence to the Red River, two or three hundred crofters from the Highlands and the Orkneys. A little later these were joined by some Swiss soldiers of fortune who had fought for Canada in the War of 1812. But Selkirk had reckoned without the partners of the North-West Company of Montreal, who were not prepared to permit mere herders and tillers to disturb the Indians and the game. The Nor'Westers attacked the helpless colonists and massacred a score of them. Selkirk retorted in kind, leading out an armed band which seized the Nor'Westers' chief post at Fort William. The war was then transferred to the courts, with heart-breaking delays and endless expense. At last Selkirk died broken in spirit, and most of his colonists drifted to Canada or across the border. But a handful held on, and for fifty years their little settlement on the Red River remained a solitary outpost of colonization.

Once arrived in Canada, the settler soon found that he had no primrose path before him. Canada remained for many years a land of struggling pioneers, who had little truck or trade with the world out of sight of their log shacks. The habitant on the seigneuries of Lower Canada continued to farm as his grandfather had farmed, finding his holding sufficient for his modest needs, even though divided into ever narrower ribbons as *le bon Dieu* sent more and yet more sons to share the heritage. The English-speaking settler, equipped with ax and sickle and flail, with spinning wheel and iron kettle, lived a life almost equally primitive and self-contained. He and his good wife grew the wheat, the corn, and the potatoes, made the soap and the candles, the maple sugar and the "yarbs," the deerskin shoes and the homespun cloth that met their needs. They had little to buy and little to sell. In spite of the preference which Great Britain gave Canadian grain, in return for the preference exacted on British manufactured goods, practically no wheat was exported until the close of this period. The barrels of potash and pearl-ash leached out from the ashes of the splendid hardwood trees which he burned as enemies were the chief source of ready money for the back-woods settler. The one substantial export of the colonies came, not from the farmer's clearing, but from the forest. Great rafts of square pine timber were floated down the Ottawa or the St. John every spring to be loaded for England. The lumberjack lent picturesqueness to the land-scape and the vocabulary and circulated ready money, but his industry did little directly to ad-vance permanent settlement or the wise use of Canadian resources.

The self-contained life of each community and each farm pointed to the lack of good means of transport. New Brunswick and the Canadas were fortunate in the possession of great lake and river systems, but these were available only in summer and were often impeded by falls and rapids. On

these waters the Indian bark canoe had given way
to the French bateau, a square-rigged flat-bot-
tomed boat, and after the war the bateau shared
the honors with the larger Durham boat brought
in from "the States."

Canadians took their full share in developing
steamship transportation. In 1809, two years after
Fulton's success on the Hudson, John Molson built
and ran a steamer between Montreal and Quebec.
The first vessel to cross the Atlantic wholly under
steam, the *Royal William*, was built in Quebec and
sailed from that port in 1833. Following and rival-
ing American enterprise, side-wheelers, marvels of
speed and luxury for the day, were put on the lakes
in the thirties. Canals were built, the Lachine
in 1821–25, the Welland around Niagara Falls in
1824–29, and the Rideau, as a military undertaking, in 1826–32, all in response to the stimulus
given by De Witt Clinton, who had begun the "Erie
Ditch" in 1817. On land, road making made slower
progress. The blazed trail gave way to the cor-
duroy road, and the pack horse to the oxcart or the
stage. Upper Canada had the honor of inventing,
in 1835, the plank road, which for some years thereafter became the fashion through the forested States
to the south. But at best neither roads nor vehicles

were fitted for carrying large loads from inland
farms to waterside markets.

Money and banks were as necessary to develop
intercourse as roads and canals. Until after the
War of 1812, when army gold and army bills ran
freely, money was rare and barter served pioneer
needs. For many years after the war a jumble of
English sovereigns and shillings, of Spanish dollars,
French crowns, and American silver, made up the
currency in use, circulating sometimes by weight
and sometimes by tale, at rates that were constantly shifting. The position of the colonies as a
link between Great Britain and the United States
was curiously illustrated in the currency system.
The motley jumble of coins in use were rated in
Halifax currency, a mere money of account or
bookkeeping standard, with no actual coins to
correspond, adapted to both English and United
States currency systems. The unit was the pound,
divided into shillings and pence as in England,
but the pound was made equal to four dollars in
American money; it took £1 4s. 4d. in Halifax
currency to make £1 sterling. Still more curious
was the influence of American banking. Montreal
merchants in 1808 took up the ideas of Alexander
Hamilton and after several vain attempts founded

the Bank of Montreal in 1817, with those features of government charter, branch banks, and restrictions as to the proportion of debts to capital and the holding of real property which had marked Hamilton's plan. But while Canadian banks, one after another, were founded on the same model and throughout adhered to an asset-secured currency basis, Hamilton's own country abandoned his ideas, usually for the worse.

In the social life of the cities the influence of the official classes and, in Halifax and Quebec, of the British redcoats stationed there was all pervading. In the country the pioneers took what diversions a hard life permitted. There were "bees" and "frolics," ranging from strenuous barn raisings, with heavy drinking and fighting, to mild apple parings or quilt patchings. There were the visits of the Yankee peddler with his "notions," his welcome pack, and his gossip. Churches grew, thanks in part to grants of government land or old endowments or gifts from missionary societies overseas, but more to the zeal of lay preachers and circuit riders. Schools fared worse. In Lower Canada there was an excellent system of classical schools for the priests and professional classes, and there were numerous convents which taught the girls, but the habitants were for the most part quite untouched by book learning. In Upper Canada grammar schools and academies were founded with commendable promptness, and a common school system was established in 1816, but grants were niggardly and compulsion was lacking. Even at the close of the thirties only one child in seven was in school, and he was, as often as not, committed to the tender mercies of some broken-down pensioner or some ancient tippler who could barely sign his mark. There was but little administrative control by the provincial authorities. The textbooks in use came largely from the United States and glorified that land and all its ways in the best Fourth-of-July manner, to the scandal of the loyal elect. The press was represented by a few weekly newspapers; only one daily existed in Upper Canada before 1840.

Against this background there developed during the period 1815-41 a tense constitutional struggle which was to exert a profound influence on the making of the nation. The stage on which the drama was enacted was a small one, and the actors were little known to the world of their day, but the drama had an interest of its own and no little significance for the future.

In one aspect the struggle for self-government in British North America was simply a local manifestation of a world-wide movement which found more notable expression in other lands. After a troubled dawn, democracy was coming to its own. In England the black reaction which had identified all proposals for reform with treasonable sympathy for bloodstained France was giving way, and the middle classes were about to triumph in the great franchise reform of 1832. In the United States, after a generation of conservatism, Jacksonian democracy was to sweep all before it. These developments paralleled and in some measure influenced the movement of events in the British North American provinces. But this movement had a color of its own. The growth of self-government in an independent country was one thing; in a colony owing allegiance to a supreme Parliament overseas, it was quite another. The task of the provinces — not solved in this period, it is true, but squarely faced — was to reconcile democracy and empire.

The people of the Canadas in 1791, and of the provinces by the sea a little earlier, had been given the right to elect one house of the legislature. More than this instalment of self-government the authorities were not prepared to grant. The people, or rather the property holders among them, might be entrusted to vote taxes and appropriations, to present grievances, and to take a share in legislation. They could not, however, be permitted to control the Government, because, to state an obvious fact, they could not govern themselves as well as their betters could rule them. Besides, if the people of a colony did govern themselves, what would become of the rights and interests of the mother country? What would become of the Empire itself?

What was the use and object of the Empire? In brief, according to the theory and practice then in force, the end of empire was the profit which comes from trade; the means was the political subordination of the colonies to prevent interference with this profit; and the debit entry set against this profit was the cost of the diplomacy, the armaments, and the wars required to hold the overseas possessions against other powers. The policy was still that which had been set forth in the preamble of the Navigation Act of 1663, ensuring the mother country the sole right to sell European wares in its colonies: "the maintaining a greater correspondence and kindnesse between them [the subjects at

home and those in the plantations] and keeping
them in a firmer dependence upon it [the mother
country], and rendering them yet more beneficial
and advantageous unto it in the further Imploy-
ment and Encrease of English Shipping and Sea-
men, and vent of English Woollen and other Manufactures and Commodities rendering the Navigation to and from the same more safe and cheape,
and makeing this Kingdom a Staple not only of the
Commodities of those Plantations but also of the
Commodities of other countries and places for the
supplying of them, and it being the usage of other
Nations to keep their [plantation] Trade to themselves." Adam Smith had raised a doubt as to the
wisdom of the end. The American Revolution had
raised a doubt as to the wisdom of the means. Yet,
with significant changes, the old colonial system
lasted for full two generations after 1776.

In the second British Empire, which rose after
the loss of the first in 1783, the means to the old
end were altered. To secure control and to prevent disaffection and democratic folly, the authorities relied not merely on their own powers but on
the coöperation of friendly classes and interests
in the colonies themselves. Their direct control
was exercised in many ways. In last reserve there

was the supreme authority of King and Parliament to bind the colonies by treaty and by law and the right to veto any colonial enactment. This was as before the Revolution. One change lay in the renunciation in 1778 of the intention to use the supreme legislative power to levy taxes, though the right to control the fiscal system of the colonies in conformity with imperial policy was still claimed and practised. In fact, far from seeking to secure a direct revenue, the British Government was more than content to pay part of the piper's fee for the sake of being able to call the tune. "It is considered by the Well wishers of Government," wrote Milnes, Lieutenant Governor of Lower Canada, in 1800, "as a fortunate Circumstance that the Revenue is not at present equal to the Expenditure." A further change came in the minute control exercised by the Colonial Office, or rather by the permanent clerks who, in Charles Buller's phrase, were really "Mr. Mother Country." The Governor was the local agent of the Colonial Office. He acted on its instructions and was responsible to it, and to it alone, for the exercise of the wide administrative powers entrusted to him.

But all these powers, it was believed, would fail in their purpose if democracy were allowed to grow unchecked in the colonies themselves. It was an essential part of the colonial policy of the time to build up conservative social forces among the people and to give a controlling voice in the local administration to a nominated and official class. It has been seen that the statesmen of 1791 looked to a nominated executive and legislative council, an hereditary aristocracy, and an established church, to keep the colony in hand. British legislation fostered and supported a ruling class in the colonies, and in turn this class was to support British connection and British control. How this policy, half avowed and half unconscious, worked out in each of the provinces must now be recorded.

In Upper Canada party struggles did not take shape until well after the War of 1812. At the founding of the colony the people had been very much of one temper and one condition. In time, however, divergences appeared and gradually hardened into political divisions. A governing class, or rather clique, was the first to become differentiated. Its emergence was slower than in New Brunswick, for instance, since Upper Canada had received few of the Loyalists who were distinguished by social position or political experience.

In time a group was formed by the accident of occupation, early settlement, residence in the little town of York, the capital after 1794, the holding of office, or by some advantage in wealth or education or capacity which in time became cumulative. The group came to be known as the Family Compact. There had been, in fact, no intermarriage among its members beyond what was natural in a small and isolated community, but the phrase had a certain appositeness. They were closely linked by loyalty to Church and King, by enmity to republics and republicans, by the memory of the sacrifice and peril they or their fathers had shared, and by the conviction that the province owed them the best living it could bestow. This living they succeeded in collecting. "The bench, the magistracy, the high officials of the established church, and a great part of the legal profession," declared Lord Durham in 1839, "are filled by the adherents of this party; by grant or purchase they have acquired nearly the whole of the waste lands of the province; they are all-powerful in the chartered banks, and till lately shared among themselves almost exclusively all offices of trust and profit." Fortunately the last absurdity of creating Dukes of Toronto and Barons of Niagara Falls was never carried through, or rather was postponed a full century; but this touch was scarcely needed to give the clique its cachet. The ten-year governorship of Sir Peregrine Maitland (1818–28), a most punctilious person, gave the finishing touches to this backwoods aristocracy.

The great majority of the group, men of the Scott and Boulton, Sherwood and Hagerman and Allan MacNab types, had nothing but their prejudices to distinguish them, but two of their number were of outstanding capacity. John Beverley Robinson, Attorney General from 1819 to 1829 and thereafter for over thirty years Chief Justice, was a true aristocrat, distrustful of the rabble, but as honest and high-minded as he was able, seeking his country's gain, as he saw it, not his own. A more rugged and domineering character, equally certain of his right to rule and less squeamish about the means, was John Strachan, afterwards Bishop of Toronto. Educated a Presbyterian, he had come to Canada from Aberdeen as a dominie but had remained as an Anglican clergyman in a capacity promising more advancement. His abounding vigor and persistence soon made him the dominant force in the Church, and with a convert's zeal he labored to give it exclusive place and power.

The opposition to the Family Compact was of a more motley hue, as is the way with oppositions. Opposition became potential when new settlers poured into the province from the United States or overseas, marked out from their Loyalist forerunners not merely by differences of political background and experience but by differences in religion. The Church of England had been dominant among the Loyalists; but the newcomers were chiefly Methodist and Presbyterian. Opposition became actual with the rise of concrete and acute grievances and with the appearance of leaders who voiced the growing discontent.

The political exclusiveness of the Family Compact did not rouse resentment half as deep as did their religious, or at least denominational, pretensions. The refusal of the Compact to permit Methodist ministers to perform the marriage ceremony was not soon forgotten. There were scores of settlements where no clergyman of the Established Church of England or of Scotland resided, and marriages here had been of necessity performed by other ministers. A bill passed the Assembly in 1824 legalizing such marriages in the past and giving the required authority for the future; and when it was rejected by the Legislative

Council, resentment flamed high. An attempt of Strachan to indict the loyalty of practically all but the Anglican clergy intensified this feeling; and the critics went on to call in question the claims of his Church to establishment and landed endowment.

The land question was the most serious that faced the province. The administration of those in power was condemned on three distinct counts. The granting of land to individuals had been lavish; it had been lax; and it had been marked by gross favoritism. By 1824, when the population was only 150,000, some 11,000,000 acres had been granted; ninety years later, when the population was 2,700,000, the total amount of improved land was only 13,000,000 acres. Moreover the attempt to use vast areas of the Crown Lands to endow solely the Anglican Church roused bitter jealousies. Yet even these grievances paled in actual hardship beside the results of holding the vast waste areas unimproved. What with Crown Reserves, Clergy Reserves, grants to those who had served the state, and holdings picked up by speculators from soldiers or poorer Loyalists for a few pounds or a few gallons of whisky, millions of acres were held untenanted and unimproved, waiting for a rise in value as a consequence of the toil of settlers on neighboring farms. Not one-tenth of the lands granted were occupied by the persons to whom they had been assigned. The province had given away almost all its vast heritage, and more than nine-tenths of it was still in wilderness. These speculative holdings made immensely more difficult every common neighborhood task. At best the machinery and the money for building roads, bridges, and schools were scanty, but with these unimproved reserves thrust in between the scattered shacks, the task was disheartening. "The reserve of two-sevenths of the land for the Crown and clergy," declared the township of Sandwich in 1817, "must for a long time keep the country a wilderness, a harbour for wolves, a hindrance to a compact and good neighborhood."

A further source of discontent developed in the disabilities affecting recent American settlers. A court decision in 1824 held that no one who had resided in the United States after 1783 could possess or transmit British citizenship, with which went the right to inherit real estate. This decision bore heavily upon thousands of "late Loyalists" and more recent incomers. Under the instructions of the Colonial Office, a remedial bill was introduced in the Legislative Council in 1827, but it was a grudging, halfway measure which the Assembly refused to accept. After several sessions of quarreling, the Assembly had its way; but in the meantime the men affected had been driven into permanent and active opposition.

The leaders of the movement of resistance which now began to gather force included all sorts and conditions of men. The fiercest and most aggressive were two Scotchmen, Robert Gourlay and William Lyon Mackenzie. Gourlay, one of those restless and indispensable cranks who make the world turn round, active, obstinate, imprudent, uncompromisingly devoted to the common good as he saw it, came to Canada in 1817 on settlement and colonization bent. Innocent inquiries which he sent broadcast as to the condition of the province gave the settlers an opportunity for voicing their pent-up discontent, and soon Gourlay was launched upon the sea of politics. Mackenzie, who came to Canada three years later, was a born agitator, fearless, untiring, a good hater, master of a vitriolic vocabulary, and absolutely unpurchasable. He found his vein in weekly journalism, and for nearly forty years was the stormy petrel of Canadian politics. From England there came, among others, Dr. John Rolph, shrewd and politic, and Captain John Matthews, a half-pay artillery officer. Peter Perry, downright and rugged and of a homely eloquence, represented the Loyalists of the Bay of Quinté, which was the center of Canadian Methodism. Among the newer comers from the United States, the foremost were Barnabas Bidwell, who had been Attorney General of Massachusetts but had fled to Canada in 1810 when accused of misappropriating public money, and his son, Marshall Spring Bidwell, one of the ablest and most single-minded men who ever entered Canadian public life. From Ireland came Dr. William Warren Baldwin, whose son Robert, born in Canada, was less surpassingly able than the younger Bidwell but equally moderate and equally beyond suspicion of faction or self-seeking.

How were these men to bring about the reform which they desired? Their first aim was obviously to secure a majority in the Assembly, and by the election of 1828 they attained this first object. But the limits of the power of the Assembly they soon discovered. Without definite leadership, with no control over the Administration, and with even legislative power divided, it could effect little. It was in part disappointment at the failure of the Assembly that accounted for the defeat of the

Reformers in 1830, though four years later this verdict was again reversed. Clearly the form of government itself should be changed. But in what way? Here a divergence in the ranks of the Reformers became marked. One party, looking upon the United States as the utmost achievement in democracy, proposed to follow its example in making the upper house elective and thus to give the people control of both branches of the Legislature. Another group, of whom Robert Baldwin was the chief, saw that this change would not suffice. In the States the Executive was also elected by the people. Here, where the Governor would doubtless continue to be appointed by the Crown, some other means must be found to give the people full control. Baldwin found it in the British Cabinet system, which gave real power to ministers having the confidence of a majority in Parliament. The Governor would remain, but he would be only a figurehead, a constitutional monarch acting, like the King, only on the advice of his constitutional advisers. Responsible government was Baldwin's one and absorbing idea, and his persistence led to its ultimate adoption, along with a proposal for an elective Council, in the Reform party's programme in 1834. Delay in affecting this reform, Baldwin told the Governor a year later, was "the great and all absorbing grievance before which all others sank into insignificance." The remedy could be applied "without in the least entrenching upon the just and necessary prerogatives of the Crown, which I consider, when administered by the Lieutenant Governor through the medium of a provincial ministry responsible to the provincial parliament, to be an essential part of the constitution of the province." In brief, Baldwin insisted that Simcoe's rhetorical outburst in 1791, when he declared that Upper Canada was "a perfect Image and Transcript of the British Government and Constitution," should be made effective in practice.

The course of the conflict between the Compact and the Reformers cannot be followed in detail. It had elements of tragedy, as when Gourlay was hounded into prison, where he was broken in health and shattered in mind, and then exiled from the province for criticism of the Government which was certainly no more severe than now appears every day in Opposition newspapers. The conflict had elements of the ludicrous, too, as when Captain Matthews was ordered by his military superiors to return to England because in the unrestrained festivities of New Year's Eve he had

called on a strolling troupe to play *Yankee Doodle*
and had shouted to the company, "Hats off"; or
when Governor Maitland overturned fourteen feet
of the Brock Monument to remove a copy of Mackenzie's journal, the *Colonial Advocate*, which had
inadvertently been included in the corner stone.

The weapons of the Reformers were the platform, the press, and investigations and reports
by parliamentary committees. The Compact hit
back in its own way. Every critic was denounced
as a traitor. Offending editors were put in the
pillory. Mackenzie was five times expelled from
the House, only to be returned five times by his
stubborn supporters. Matters were at a deadlock,
and it became clear either that the British Parliament, which alone could amend the Constitution,
must intervene or else that the Reformers would
be driven to desperate paths. But before matters came to this pass, an acute crisis had arisen
in Lower Canada which had its effect on all
the provinces.

In Lower Canada, the conflict which had been
smoldering before the war had since then burst into
flame. The issues of this conflict were more clear-
cut than in any of the other provinces. A coherent

opposition had formed earlier, and from beginning to end it dominated the Assembly. The governing forces were outwardly much the same as in Upper Canada — a Lieutenant Governor responsible to the Colonial Office, an Executive Council appointed by the Crown but coming to have the independent power of a well-entrenched bureaucracy, and a Legislative Council nominated by the Crown and, until nearly the end of the period, composed chiefly of the same men who served in the Executive. The little clique in control had much less popular backing than the Family Compact of Upper Canada and were of lower caliber. Robert Christie, an English-speaking member of the Assembly, who may be counted an unprejudiced witness since he was four times expelled by the majority in that house, refers to the real rulers of the province as "a few rapacious, overbearing, and irresponsible officials, without stake or other connexion in the country than their interests." At their head stood Jonathan Sewell, a Massachusetts Loyalist who had come to Lower Canada by way of New Brunswick in 1789, and who for over forty years as Attorney General, Chief Justice, or member of Executive and Legislative Councils, was the power behind the throne.

The opposition to the bureaucrats at first included both English and French elements, but the English minority were pulled in contrary ways. Their antecedents were not such as to lead them to accept meekly either the political or the social pretensions of the "Château Clique"; the American settlers in the Eastern Townships, and the Scotch and American merchants who were building up Quebec and Montreal, had called for self-government, not government from above. Yet their racial and religious prejudices were strong and made them unwilling to accept in place of the bureaucrats the dominance of an unprogressive habitant majority. The first leader of the opposition which developed in the Assembly after the War of 1812 was James Stuart, the son of the leading Anglican clergyman of his day, but he soon fell away and became a mainstay of the bureaucracy. His brother Andrew, however, kept up for many years longer a more disinterested fight. Another Scot, John Neilson, editor of the Quebec *Gazette*, was until 1833 foremost among the assailants of the bureaucracy. But steadily, as the extreme nationalist claims of the French-speaking majority provoked reprisals and as the conviction grew upon the minority that they would never be anything but a minority,[1] most of them accepted clique rule as a lesser evil than "rule by priest and demagogue."

In the reform movement in Upper Canada there were a multiplicity of leaders and a constant shifting of groups. In Lower Canada, after the defection of James Stuart in 1817, there was only one leader, Louis Joseph Papineau. For twenty years Papineau was the uncrowned king of the province. His commanding figure, his powers of oratory, outstanding in a race of orators, his fascinating manners, gave him an easy mastery over his people. Prudence did not hamper his flights; compromise was a word not found in his vocabulary. Few men have been better equipped for the agitator's task.

His father, Joseph Papineau, though of humble birth, had risen high in the life of the province. He had won distinction in his profession as a notary, as a speaker in the Assembly, and as a soldier in the defense of Quebec against the American invaders of 1775. In 1804 he had purchased

[1] The natural increase of the French-Canadian race under British rule is one of the most extraordinary phenomena in social history. The following figures illustrate the rate of that increase: the number was 16,417 in 1706; 69,810 in 1765; 479,288 in 1825; 697,084 in 1844. The population of Canada East or Lower Canada in 1844 was made up as follows: French Canadians, 524,244; English Canadians, 85,660; English, 11,895; Irish, 43,982; Scotch, 13,393; Americans, 11,946; born in other countries, 1329; place of birth not specified, 4635.

the seigneury of La Petite Nation, far up the Ottawa. Louis Joseph Papineau followed in his father's footsteps. Born in 1786, he served loyally and bravely in the War of 1812. In the same year he entered the Assembly and made his place at a single stroke. Barely three years after his election, he was chosen Speaker, and with a brief break he held that post for over twenty years.

Papineau did not soon or lightly begin his crusade against the Government. For the first five years of his Speakership, he confined himself to the routine duties of his office. As late as 1820 he pronounced a glowing eulogy on the Constitution which Great Britain had granted the province. In that year he tested the extent of the privileges so granted by joining in the attempt of the Assembly to assert its full control of the purse; but it was not until the project of uniting the two Canadas had made clear beyond dispute the hostility of the governing powers that he began his unrelenting warfare against them.

There was much to be said for a reunion of the two Canadas. The St. Lawrence bound them together, though Acts of Parliament had severed them. Upper Canada, as an inland province, restricted in its trade with its neighbor to the south, was dependent upon Lower Canada for access to the outer world. Its share of the duties collected at the Lower Canada ports until 1817 had been only one-eighth, afterwards increased to one-fifth. This inequality proved a constant source of friction. The crying necessity of coöperation for the improvement of the St. Lawrence waterway gave further ground for the contention that only by a reunion of the two provinces could efficiency be secured. In Upper Canada the Reformers were in favor of this plan, but the Compact, fearful of any disturbance of their vested interests, tended to oppose it. In Lower Canada the chief support came from the English element. The governing clique, as the older established body, had no doubt that they could bring the western section under their sway in case of union. But the main reason for their advocacy was the desire to swamp the French Canadians by an English majority. Sewell, the chief supporter of the project, frankly took this ground. The Governor, Lord Dalhousie, and the Colonial Office adopted his view; and in 1822 an attempt was made to rush a Union Bill through the British Parliament without any notice to those most concerned. It was blocked for the moment by the opposition of a Whig group led by Burdett and Mackintosh; and then Papineau and Neilson sailed to London and succeeded in inducing the Ministry to stay its hand. The danger was averted; but Papineau had become convinced that if his people were to retain the rights given them by their "Sacred Charter" they would have to fight for them. If they were to save their power, they must increase it.

How could this be done? Baldwin's bold and revolutionary policy of making the Executive responsible to the Assembly did not seem within the range of practical politics. It meant in practice the abandonment of British control, and this the Colonial Office was not willing to grant. Antoine Panet and other Assembly leaders had suggested in 1815 that it would be well, "if it were possible, to grant a number of places as Councillors or other posts of honour and of profit to those who have most influence over the majority in the Assembly, to hold so long as they maintained this influence," and James Stuart urged the same tentative suggestion a year later. But even before this the Colonial Office had made clear its position. "His Majesty's Government," declared the Colonial Secretary, Lord Bathurst, in 1814, "never can admit so novel & inconvenient a Principle as that of allowing the

Governor of a Colony to be divested of his responsibility [to the Colonial Office] for the acts done during his administration or permit him to shield himself under the advice of any Persons, however respectable, either from their character or their Office."

Two other courses had the sanction of precedent, one of English, the other of American example. The English House of Commons had secured its dominant place in the government of the country by its control of the purse. Why should not the Assembly do likewise? One obvious difficulty lay in the fact that the Assembly was not the sole authority in raising revenue. The British Parliament had retained the power to levy certain duties as part of its system of commercial control, and other casual and territorial dues lay in the right of the Crown. From 1820, therefore, the Assembly's main aim was twofold — to obtain control of these remaining sources of revenue, and by means of this power to bludgeon the Legislative Council and the Governor into compliance with its wishes. The Colonial Office made concessions, offering to resign all its taxing powers in return for a permanent civil list, that is, an assurance that the salaries of the chief officials would not be questioned annually. The offer was reasonable in itself but, as it would have hampered the full use of the revenue bludgeon, it was scornfully declined.

The other aim of the *Patriotes*, as the Opposition styled themselves, was to conquer the Legislative Council by making it elective. Papineau, in spite of his early prejudices, was drawn more and more into sympathy with the form of democracy worked out in the United States. In fact, he not only looked to it as a model but, as the thirties wore on, he came to hope that moral, if not physical, support might be found there for his campaign against the English Government. After 1830 the demand for an elective Legislative Council became more and more insistent.

The struggle soon reached a deadlock. Governor followed Governor: Lord Dalhousie, Sir James Kempt, Lord Aylmer, all in turn failed to allay the storm. The Assembly raised its claims each session and fulminated against all the opposing powers in windy resolutions. Papineau, embittered by continued opposition, carried away by his own eloquence, and steadied by no responsibility of office, became more implacable in his demands. Many of his moderate supporters — Neilson, Andrew Stuart, Quesnel, Cuvillier — fell

away, only to be overwhelmed in the first election
at a wave of the great tribune's hand. Business was
blocked, supplies were not voted, and civil servants
made shift without salary as best they could.

The British Government awoke, or half awoke,
to the seriousness of the situation. In 1835 a
Royal Commission of three, with the new Governor General, Lord Gosford, as chairman, was appointed to make inquiries and to recommend a
policy. Gosford, a genial Irishman, showed himself most conciliatory in both private intercourse
and public discourse. Unfortunately the rash act
of the new Lieutenant Governor of Upper Canada,
Sir Francis Bond Head, in publishing the instructions of the Colonial Office, showed that the policy
of Downing Street was the futile one of conciliation without concession. The Assembly once more
refused to grant supplies without redress of grievances. The Commissioners made their report opposing any substantial change. In March, 1837,
Lord John Russell, Chancellor of the Exchequer
in the Melbourne Ministry, opposed only by a
handful of Radical and Irish members, carried
through the British Parliament a series of resolutions authorizing the Governor to take from the
Treasury without the consent of the Assembly the

funds needed for civil administration, offering control of all revenues in return for a permanent civil list, and rejecting absolutely the demands alike for a responsible Executive and for an elective Council.

British statesmanship was bankrupt. Its final answer to the demands for redress was to stand pat. Papineau, without seeing what the end would be, held to his course. Younger men, carried away by the passions he had aroused, pushed on still more recklessly. If reform could not be obtained within the British Empire, it must be sought by setting up an independent republic on the St. Lawrence or by annexation to the United States.

In Upper Canada, at the same time, matters had come to the verge of rebellion. Sir John Colborne had, just before retiring as Lieutenant Governor in 1836, added fuel to the flames by creating and endowing some forty-four rectories, thus strengthening the grip of the Anglican Church on the province. His successor, Sir Francis Bond Head, was a man of such rash and unbalanced judgment as to lend support to the tradition that he was appointed by mistake for his cousin, Edmund Head, who was made Governor of United Canada twenty years later. He appointed to his Executive Council three Reformers, Baldwin, Rolph, and Dunn, only to make clear by his refusal to consult them his inability to understand their demand for responsible government. All the members of the Executive Council thereupon resigned, and the Assembly refused supplies. Head dissolved the House and appealed to the people.

The weight of executive patronage, the insistence of the Governor that British connection was at stake, the alarms caused by some injudicious statements of Mackenzie and his Radical ally in England, Joseph Hume, and the defection of the Methodists, whose leader, Egerton Ryerson, had quarreled with Mackenzie, resulted in the overwhelming defeat of the Reformers. The sting of defeat, the failure of the Family Compact to carry out their eleventh hour promises of reform, and the passing of Lord John Russell's reactionary resolutions convinced a section of the Reform party, in Upper Canada as well as in Lower Canada, that an appeal to force was the only way out.

Toward the end of 1837 armed rebellion broke out in both the Canadas. In both it was merely a flash in the pan. In Lower Canada there had been latterly much use of the phrases of revolution and some drilling, but rebellion was neither definitely planned nor carefully organized. The more extreme leaders of the *Patriotes* simply drifted into it, and the actual outbreak was a haphazard affair. Alarmed by the sudden and seemingly concerted departure of Papineau and some of his lieutenants, Nelson, Brown, and O'Callaghan, from Montreal, the Government gave orders for their arrest. The petty skirmish that followed on November 16, 1837, was the signal for the rallying of armed habitants around impromptu leaders at various points. The rising was local and spasmodic. The vast body of the habitants stood aloof. The Catholic Church, which earlier had sympathized with Papineau, had parted from him when he developed radical and republican views. Now the strong exhortations of the clergy to the faithful counted for much in keeping peace, and in one view justified the policy of the British Government in seeking to purchase their favor. The Quebec and Three Rivers districts remained quiet. In the Richelieu and Montreal districts, where disaffection was strongest, the habitants lacked leadership, discipline, and touch with other groups, and were armed only with old flintlocks, scythes, or clubs. Here and there a brave and skillful leader, such as Dr. Jean Olivier Chénier, was thrown up by the

stress, and in more than one skirmish the habitants fought bravely, but from the start the rising
was doomed. British regulars supported by English and French volunteers speedily stamped it
out. The leaders fled to the United States or were
made prisoners, and in a brief three weeks the
fighting was over.

In Upper Canada there was more deliberate planning and careful organization but even less popular
support. Mackenzie, with Rolph and Duncombe
as his chief supporters, organized committees
throughout the province. Early in December, his
hand forced by the outbreak in Lower Canada,
Mackenzie with less than a thousand followers
endeavored to seize Toronto, the seat of government. The province was stripped of regular
troops, and the Governor was incapable; but the
rebels, save for one old Dutch soldier of fortune,
Van Egmond, had no experienced leader. After
a stage skirmish with the loyal militia they broke
and fled. Mackenzie and Rolph escaped to the
United States. With his headquarters at Buffalo,
Mackenzie rallied a force of border desperadoes
and seized Navy Island in the Niagara River.
The border raids at this and other points kept
the province under arms for a year; but, in view

of the hostility of the greater part of the people, their would-be liberators gave up the attempt at invasion.

This border warfare came near to involving the United States and Great Britain in war. All along the boundary line American sympathy was strongly with the rebels. The Federal Government, somewhat tardily, took steps to prevent the making of its territory a base of operations against a friendly country; but the state Governments were lax, and the general public was openly eager to see the British flag hauled down. Raiding parties collected and crossed the border without being molested, and arms from state arsenals found their way into the raiders' hands. But when a Canadian militia force crossed the Niagara, and cut out and burned a steamer which was moored to the American shore and which was supplying the rebels on Navy Island, killing one member of the crew, an outburst of popular indignation flared out against such a violation of neutrality. Later, in 1841, when Alexander McLeod, a Canadian who had boasted that he had been one of the cutting-out party, was arrested in New York State and tried for murder, feeling once more rose high, but fortunately the discharge of McLeod for lack of evidence opened a way out of the difficult situation. A year later Peel and Webster, representing the two countries, exchanged formal explanations, and the incident was closed.

In Upper Canada many a rebel sympathizer lay for months in jail, but only two leaders, Lount and Matthews, both brave men, paid the penalty of death for their failure. In Lower Canada the new Governor General, Lord Durham, proved more clement, merely banishing to Bermuda eight of the captured leaders. When, a year later, after Durham's return to England, a second brief rising broke out under Robert Nelson, it was stamped out in a week, twelve of the ringleaders were executed, and others were deported to Botany Bay.

The rebellion, it seemed, had failed and failed miserably. Most of the leaders of the extreme factions in both provinces had been discredited, and the moderate men had been driven into the government camp. Yet in one sense the rising proved successful. It was not the first nor the last time that wild and misguided force brought reform where sane and moderate tactics met only contempt. If men were willing to die to redress their wrongs, the most easy-going official could no longer deny that there was a case for inquiry and possibly for reform.

Lord Melbourne's Government had acted at once in sending out to Canada, as Governor General and High Commissioner with sweeping powers, one of the ablest men in English public life. Lord Durham was an aristocratic Radical, intensely devoted to political equality and equally convinced of his own personal superiority. Yet he had vision, firmness, independence, and his very rudeness kept him free from the social influences which had ensnared many another Governor. Attended by a gorgeous retinue and by some able working secretaries, including Charles Buller, Carlyle's pupil, he made a rapid survey of Upper and Lower Canada. Suddenly, after five crowded months, his mission ended. He had left at home active enemies and lukewarm friends. Lord Brougham, one of his foes, called in question the legality of his edict banishing the rebel leaders to Bermuda. The Ministers did not back him, as they should have done; and Durham indignantly resigned and hurried back to England.

Three months later, however, his *Report* appeared and his mission stood vindicated. There are few British state papers of more fame or more worth than Durham's *Report*. It was not, however, the beginning and the end of wisdom in colonial policy, as has often been declared. Much that Durham advocated was not new, and much has been condemned by time. His main suggestions were four: to unite the Canadas, to swamp the French Canadians by such union, to grant a measure of responsible government, and to set up municipal government. His attitude towards the French Canadians was prejudiced and shortsighted. He was not the first to recommend responsible government, nor did his approval make it a reality. Yet with all qualifications his *Report* showed a confidence in the liberating and solving power of self-government which was the all-essential thing for the English Government to see; and his reasoned and powerful advocacy gave an impetus and a rallying point to the movement which were to prove of the greatest value in the future growth not only of Canada but of the whole British Empire.

CHAPTER III

THE UNION ERA

THE struggle for self-government seemed to have ended in deadlock and chaos. Yet under the wreckage new lines of constructive effort were forming. The rebellion had at least proved that the old order was doomed. For half a century the attempt had been made to govern the Canadas as separate provinces and with the half measure of freedom involved in representative government. For the next quarter of a century the experiment of responsible government together with union of the two provinces was to be given its trial.

The union of the two provinces was the phase of Durham's policy which met fullest acceptance in England. It was not possible, in the view of the British Ministry, to take away permanently from the people of Lower Canada the measure of self-government involved in permitting them to choose their representatives in a House of Assembly. It

was equally impossible, they considered, to permit
a French-Canadian majority ever again to bring
all government to a standstill. The only solution
of the problem was to unite the two provinces and
thus swamp the French Canadians by an English
majority. Lower Canada, Durham had insisted,
must be made "an English province." Sooner or
later the French Canadians must lose their separate nationality; and it was, he contended, the
part of statesmanship to make it sooner. Union,
moreover, would make possible a common financial policy and an energetic development of the
resources of both provinces.

This was the first task set Durham's successor,
Charles Poulett Thomson, better known as Lord
Sydenham. Like Durham he was a man of outstanding capacity. The British Government had
learned at last to send men of the caliber the emergency demanded. Like Durham he was a wealthy
Radical politician, but there the resemblance ended.
Where Durham played the dictator, Sydenham preferred to intrigue and to manage men, to win them
by his adroitness and to convince them by his energy and his business knowledge. He was well fitted for the transition tasks before him, though too
masterful to fill the rôle of ornamental monarch

which the advocates of responsible government had cast for the Governor.

Sydenham reached Canada in October, 1839. With the assistance of James Stuart, now a baronet and Chief Justice of Lower Canada, he drafted a union measure. In Lower Canada the Assembly had been suspended, and the Special Council appointed in its stead accepted the bill without serious demur. More difficulty was found in Upper Canada, where the Family Compact, still entrenched in the Legislative Council, feared the risk to their own position that union would bring and shrank from the task of assimilating half a million disaffected French Canadians. But with the support of the Reformers and of the more moderate among the Family Compact party, Sydenham forced his measure through. A confirming bill passed the British Parliament; and on February 10, 1841, the Union of Canada was proclaimed.

The Act provided for the union of the two provinces, under a Governor, an appointed Legislative Council, and an elective Assembly. In the Assembly each section of the new province was to receive equal representation, though the population of Lower Canada still greatly exceeded that of Upper Canada. The Assembly was to have full control of all revenues, and in return a permanent civil list was granted. Either English or French could be used in debate, but all parliamentary journals and papers were to be printed in English only.[1]

In June, 1841, the first Parliament of united Canada met at Kingston, which as the most central point had been chosen as the new capital. Under Sydenham's shrewd and energetic leadership a business programme of long-delayed reforms was put through. A large loan, guaranteed by the British Government, made possible extensive provision for building roads, bridges, and canals around the rapids in the St. Lawrence. Municipal institutions were set up, and reforms were effected in the provincial administration.

Lord John Russell in England and Sydenham in Canada were anxious to keep the question of responsible government in the background. For the first busy months they succeeded, but the new Parliament contained men quite as strong willed as either and of quite other views. Before the

---

[1] From 1841 to 1867 the whole province was legally known as the "Province of Canada." Yet a measure of administrative separation between the old sections remained, and the terms "Canada East" and "Canada West" received official sanction. The older terms, "Lower Canada" and "Upper Canada," lingered on in popular usage

first session had begun, Baldwin and the new French-Canadian leader, La Fontaine, had raised the issue and begun a new struggle in which their single-minded devotion and unflinching courage were to attain a complete success.

Responsible government was in 1841 only a phrase, a watchword. Its full implications became clear only after many years. It meant three things: cabinet government, self-government, and party government. It meant that the government of the country should be carried on by a Cabinet or Executive Council, all members of Parliament, all belonging to the party which had the majority in the Assembly, and under the leadership of a Prime Minister, the working head of the Government. The nominal head, Governor or King, could act only on the advice of his ministers, who alone were held responsible to Parliament for the course of the Government. It meant, further, national self-government. The Governor could not serve two masters. If he must take the advice of his ministers in Canada, he could not take the possibly conflicting advice of ministers in London. The people of Canada would be the ultimate court of appeal. And finally, responsible government meant party government. The cabinet system presupposed a definite and united majority behind the Government. It was the business of the party system to provide that majority, to insure responsible and steady action, and at the same time responsible criticism from Her Majesty's loyal Opposition. Baldwin saw this clearly in 1841, but it took hard fighting throughout the forties to bring all his fellow countrymen to see likewise and to induce the English Government to resign itself to the prospect.

Sydenham fought against responsible government but advanced it against his will. The only sense in which he, like Russell, was prepared to concede such liberty was that the Governor should choose his advisers as far as possible from men having the confidence of the Assembly. They were to be his advisers only, in fact as well as form. The Governor was still to govern, was to be Prime Minister and Governor in one. When Baldwin, who had been given a seat in the Executive Council, demanded in 1841 that this body should be reconstructed in such a way as to include some French-Canadian members and to exclude the Family Compact men, Sydenham flatly refused. Baldwin then resigned and went into opposition, but Sydenham unwillingly played into his hand.

By choosing his council solely from members of the two Houses, he established a definite connection between Executive and Assembly and thus gave an opportunity for the discussion of the administration of policy in the House and for the forming of government and opposition parties. Before the first session closed, the majority which Sydenham had built up by acting as a party leader at the very time he was deriding parties as mere factions, crumbled away, and he was forced to accept resolutions insisting that the Governor's advisers must be men "possessed of the confidence of the representatives of the people." Fate ended his work at its height. Riding home one September evening, he was thrown from his horse and died from the injuries before the month was out.

It fell to the Tory Government of Peel to choose Sydenham's successor. They named Sir Charles Bagot, already distinguished for his career in diplomacy and known for his hand in matters which were to interest the greater Canada, the Rush-Bagot Convention with the United States and the treaty with Russia which fixed, only too vaguely, the boundaries of Alaska. He was under strict injunctions from the Colonial Secretary, Lord Stanley, to continue Sydenham's policy and to make no further concession to the demands for responsible government or party control. Yet this Tory nominee of a Tory Cabinet, in his brief term of office, insured a great advance along this very path toward freedom. His easy-going temper predisposed him to play the part of constitutional monarch rather than of Prime Minister, and in any case he faced a majority in the Assembly resolute in its determination.

The policy of swamping French influence had already proved a failure. Sydenham had given it a full trial. He had done his best, or his worst, by unscrupulous manipulation, to keep the French Canadians from gaining their fair quota of the members in the Union Assembly. Those who were elected he ignored. "They have forgotten nothing and learnt nothing by the Rebellion," he declared, "and are more unfit for representative government than they were in 1791." This was far from a true reading of the situation. The French stood aloof, it is true, a compact and sullen group, angered by the undisguised policy of Anglicization that faced them and by Sydenham's unscrupulous tactics. But they had learned restraint and had found leaders and allies of the kind most needed. Papineau's place — for the great tribune was now in exile in Paris, consorting with the republicans and socialists who were to bring about the Revolution of 1848 — had been taken by one of his former lieutenants. Louis Hippolyte La Fontaine still stands out as one of the two or three greatest Canadians of French descent, a man of massive intellect, of unquestioned integrity, and of firm but moderate temper. With Baldwin he came to form a close and lifelong friendship. The Reformers of Canada West, as Upper Canada was now called, formed a working alliance with La Fontaine which gave them a sweeping majority in the Assembly. Bagot bowed to the inevitable and called La Fontaine and Baldwin to his Council. Ill health made it impossible for him to take much part in the government, and the Council was far on the way to obtaining the unity and the independence of a true Cabinet when Bagot's death in 1843 brought a new turn in affairs.

The British Ministers had seen with growing uneasiness Bagot's concessions. His successor, Sir Charles Metcalfe, a man of honest and kindly ways but accustomed to governing oriental peoples, determined to make a stand against the pretensions of the Reformers. In this attitude he was strongly backed both by Stanley and by his successor, that brilliant young Tory, William Ewart Gladstone. Metcalfe insisted once more that the Governor must govern. While the members of the Council, as individuals, might give him advice, it was for him to decide whether or not to take it. The inevitable clash with his Ministers came in the autumn of 1843 over a question of patronage. They resigned, and after months of effort Metcalfe patched up a Ministry with W. H. Draper as the leading member. In an election in which Metcalfe himself took the platform and in which once more British connection was said to be at stake, the Ministry obtained a narrow majority. But opinion soon turned, and when Metcalfe, the third Governor in four years to whom Canada had proved fatal, went home to die, he knew that his stand had been in vain. The Ministry, after a precarious life of three years, went to the country only to be beaten by an overwhelming majority in both East and West. When, in 1848, Baldwin and La Fontaine were called to office under the new Governor General, Lord Elgin, the fight was won. Many years were to pass before the full implications of responsible government were worked out, but henceforth even the straitest Tory conceded the principle. Responsible government had ceased to be a party cry and had become the common heritage of all Canadians.

Lord Elgin, who was Durham's son-in-law, was a man well able to bear the mantle of his predecessors. Yet he realized that the day had passed when Governors could govern and was content rather to advise his advisers, to wield the personal influence that his experience and sagacity warranted. Hitherto the stages in Canadian history had been recorded by the term of office of the Governors; henceforth it was to be the tenure of Cabinets which counted. Elgin ceased even to attend the Council, and after his time the Governor became more and more the constitutional monarch, busied in laying corner stones and listening to tiresome official addresses. In emergencies, and especially in the gap or interregnum between Ministries, the personality of the Governor might count, but as a rule this power remained latent. Yet in two turning points in Canadian history, both of which had to do with the relations of Canada to the United States, Elgin was to play an important part: the Annexation Movement of 1849 and the Reciprocity Treaty of 1854.

In the struggle for responsible government, loyalty to the British Crown, loyalty of a superior and exclusive brand, had been the creed and the

war cry of the Tory party. Yet in 1849 men saw
the hot-heads of this group in Montreal stoning
a British Governor General and setting fire to the
Parliament Buildings, while a few months later
their elders issued a manifesto urging the annexation of Canada to the United States. Why this
sudden shift? Simply because the old colonial
system they had known and supported had come
to an end. The Empire had been taken to mean
racial ascendancy and trade profit. Now both the
political and the economic pillars were crumbling,
and the Empire appeared to have no further excuse
for existence.

In the past British connection had meant to
many of the English minority in Lower Canada a
means of redressing the political balance, of retain-
ing power in face of a body of French-speaking
citizens outnumbering them three or four to one.
Now that support had been withdrawn. Britain
had consented, unwillingly, to the setting up of
responsible government and the calling to office of
men who a dozen years before had been in arms
against the Queen or fleeing from the province.
This was gall and wormwood to the English. But
when the Ministry introduced, and the Assembly
passed, the Rebellion Losses Bill for compensating

those who had suffered destruction of property in
the outbreak, and when the terms were so drawn
as to make it possible, its critics charged, that
rebels as well as loyalists would be compensated,
flesh and blood could bear no more. The Governor
was pelted with rotten eggs when he came down to
the House to sign the bill, and the buildings where
Parliament had met since 1844, when the capital
had been transferred from Kingston to Montreal,
were stormed and burned by a street mob.

The anger felt against the Ministry thus turned
against the British Government. The English
minority felt like an advance guard in a hostile
country, deserted by the main forces, an Ulster
abandoned to Home Ruler and Sinn Feiner. They
turned to the south, to the other great English-
speaking Protestant people. If the older branch
of the race would not give them protection or a
share in dominance, perhaps the younger branch
could and would. As Lord Durham had suggested,
they were resolved that "Lower Canada must
be *English*, at the expense, if necessary, of not
being *British*."

But it was not only the political basis of the old
colonial system that was rudely shattered. The
economic foundations, too, were passing away, and

with them the profits of the Montreal merchants, who formed the backbone of the annexation movement. It has been seen that under this system Great Britain had aimed at setting up a self-contained empire, with a monopoly of the markets of the colonies. Now for her own sake she was sweeping away the tariff and shipping monopoly which had been built up through more than two centuries. The logic of Adam Smith, the experiments of Huskisson, the demands of manufacturers for cheap food and raw materials, the passionate campaigns of Cobden and Bright, and the rains that brought the Irish famine, at last had their effect. In 1846 Peel himself undertook the repeal of the Corn Laws. To Lower Canada this was a crushing blow. Until of late the preference given in the British market on colonial goods in return for the control of colonial trade had been of little value; but in 1843 the duties on Canadian wheat and flour had been greatly lowered, resulting in a preference over foreign grain reckoned at eighteen cents a bushel. While in appearance an extension of the old system of preference and protection, in reality this was a step toward its abandonment. For it was understood that American grain, imported into Canada at a low duty, whether shipped direct or ground into flour, would be admitted at the same low rates. The Act, by opening a backdoor to United States wheat, foreshadowed the triumph of the cheap food agitators in England. But the merchants, the millers, and the forwarders of Montreal could not believe this. The canal system was rushed through, large flour mills were built, and heavy investments of capital were made. Then in 1846 came the announcement that the artificial basis of this brief prosperity had vanished. Lord Elgin summed up the results in a dispatch in 1849: "Property in most of the Canadian towns, and more especially in the capital, has fallen fifty per cent in value within the last three years. Three-fourths of the commercial men are bankrupt, owing to free trade. A large proportion of the exportable produce of Canada is obliged to seek a market in the United States. It pays a duty of twenty per cent on the frontier. How long can such a state of things endure?"

In October, 1849, the leading men of Montreal issued a manifesto demanding annexation to the United States. A future Prime Minister of Canada, J. J. C. Abbott, four future Cabinet Ministers, John Rose, Luther Holton, D. L. Macpherson, and A. A. Dorion, and the commercial leaders of Montreal, the Molsons, Redpaths, Torrances, and Workmans, were among the signers. Besides Dorion, a few French Canadians of the *Rouge* or extreme Radical party joined in. The movement found supporters in the Eastern Townships, notably in A. T. Galt, a financier and railroad builder of distinction, and here and there in Canada West. Yet the great body of opinion was unmistakably against it. Baldwin and La Fontaine opposed it with unswerving energy, the Catholic Church in Canada East denounced it, and the rank and file of both parties in Canada West gave it short shrift. Elgin came out actively in opposition and aided in negotiating the Reciprocity Treaty with the United States which met the economic need. Montreal found itself isolated, and even there the revival of trade and the cooling of passions turned men's thoughts into other channels. Soon the movement was but a memory, chiefly serviceable to political opponents for taunting some signer of the manifesto whenever he later made parade of his loyalty. It had a more unfortunate effect, however, in leading public opinion in the United States to the belief for many years that a strong annexationist sentiment existed in Canada. Never again did annexation receive any notable measure of popular support. A national spirit was slowly gaining ground, and men were eventually to see that the alternative to looking to London for salvation was not looking to Washington but looking to themselves.

In the provinces by the sea the struggle for responsible government was won at much the same time as in Canada. The smaller field within which the contest was waged gave it a bitter personal touch; but racial hostility did not enter in, and the British Government proved less obdurate than in the western conflicts. In both Nova Scotia and New Brunswick little oligarchies had become entrenched. The Government was unprogressive, and fees and salaries were high. The Anglican Church had received privileges galling to other denominations which surpassed it in numbers. The "powers that were" found a shrewd defender in Haliburton, who tried to teach his fellow Bluenoses through the homely wit of "Sam Slick" that they should leave governing to those who had the training, the capacity, and the leisure it required. In Prince Edward Island the land question still overshadowed all others. Every proposal for its settlement was rejected by the influence of the absentee landlords in England, and the agitation went wearily on.

In Nova Scotia the outstanding figure in the ranks of reform was Joseph Howe. The son of a Loyalist settler, Howe early took to his father's work of journalism. At first his sympathies were with the governing powers, but a controversy with a brother editor, Jotham Blanchard, a New Hampshire man who found radical backing among the Scots of Pictou, gave him new light and he soon threw his whole powers into the struggle on the popular side. Howe was a man lavishly gifted, one of the most effective orators America has produced, fearing no man and no task however great, filled with a vitality, a humor, a broad sympathy for his fellows that gave him the blind obedience of thousands of followers and the glowing friendship of countless firesides. There are still old men in Nova Scotia whose proudest memory is that they once held Howe's horse or ran on an errand for a look from his kingly eye.

Howe took up the fight in earnest in 1835. The western demand for responsible government pointed the way, and Howe became, with Baldwin, its most trenchant advocate. In spite of the determined opposition of the sturdy old soldier Governor, Sir

Colin Campbell, and of his successor, Lord Falkland, who aped Sydenham and whom Howe threatened to "hire a black man to horse-whip," the reformers won. In 1848 the first responsible Cabinet in Nova Scotia came to power.

In New Brunswick the transition to responsible government came gradually and without dramatic incidents or brilliant figures on either side. Lemuel Wilmot, and later Charles Fisher, led the reform ranks, gradually securing for the Assembly control of all revenues, abolishing religious inequalities, and effecting some reform in the Executive Council, until at last in 1855 the crowning demand was tardily conceded.

From the Great Lakes to the Atlantic the political fight was won, and men turned with relief to the tasks which strife and faction had hindered. Self-government meant progressive government. With organized Cabinets coördinating and controlling their policy the provinces went ahead much faster than when Governor and Assembly stood at daggers drawn. The forties and especially the fifties were years of rapid and sound development in all the provinces, and especially in Canada West. Settlers poured in, the scattered clearings widened until one joined the next, and pioneer hardships gave way to substantial, if crude, prosperity. Education, notably under the vigorous leadership of Egerton Ryerson in Canada West, received more adequate attention. Banks grew and with them all commercial facilities increased.

The distinctive feature of this period of Canadian development, however, was the growth of canals and railroads. The forties were the time of canal building and rebuilding all along the lakes and the St. Lawrence to salt water. Canada spent millions on what were wonderful works for their day, in the hope that the St. Lawrence would become the channel for the trade of all the growing western States bordering on the Great Lakes. Scarcely were these waterway improvements completed when it was realized they had been made largely in vain. The railway had come and was outrivaling the canal. If Canadian ports and channels were even to hold their own, they must take heed of the enterprise of all the cities along the Atlantic coast of the United States, which were promoting railroads to the interior in a vigorous rivalry for the trade of the Golden West. Here was a challenge which must be taken up. The fifties became the first great railway era of Canada. In

1850 there were only sixty-six miles of railway in all the provinces; ten years later there were over two thousand. Nearly all the roads were aided by provincial or municipal bonus or guarantee. Chief among the lines was the Grand Trunk, which ran from the Detroit border to Rivière du Loup on the Gulf of St. Lawrence, and which, though it halted at that eastern terminus in the magnificent project of connecting with the railways of the Maritime Provinces, was nevertheless at that time the longest road in the world operating under single control.

The railways brought with them a new speculative fever, a more complex financial structure, a business politics which shaded into open corruption, and a closer touch with the outside world. The general substitution of steam for sail on the Atlantic during this period aided further in lessening the isolation of what had been backwoods provinces and in bringing them into closer relation with the rest of the world.

It was in closer relations with the United States that this emergence from isolation chiefly manifested itself. In the generation that followed the War of 1812 intercourse with the United States was discouraged and was remarkably insignificant.

Official policy and the memories of 1783 and 1812 alike built up a wall along the southern border. The spirit of Downing Street was shown in the instructions given to Lord Bathurst, immediately after the close of the war, to leave the territory between Montreal and Lake Champlain in a state of nature, making no further grants of land and letting the few roads which had been begun fall into decay: thus a barrier of forest wilderness would ward off republican contagion. This Chinese policy of putting up a wall of separation proved impossible to carry through, but in less extreme ways this attitude of aloofness marked the course of the Government all through the days of oversea authority.

The friction aroused by repeated boundary disputes prevented friendly relations between Canada and the United States. With unconscious irony the framers of the Peace of 1783 had prefaced their long outline of the boundaries of the United States by expressing their intention "that all disputes which might arise in future on the subject of the boundaries of the said United States may be prevented." So vague, however, were the terms of the treaty and so untrustworthy were the maps of the day that ultimately almost every clause in the boundary section gave rise to dispute.

As settlement rolled westward one section of the boundary after another came in question. Beginning in the east, the line between New Brunswick and New England was to be formed by the St. Croix River. There had been a St. Croix in Champlain's time and a St. Croix was depicted on the maps, but no river known by that name existed in 1783. The British identified it with the Schoodic, the Americans with the Magaguadavic. Arbitration in 1798 upheld the British in the contention that the Schoodic was the St. Croix but agreed with the Americans in the secondary question as to which of the two branches of the Schoodic should be followed. A similar commission in 1817 settled the dispute as to the islands in Passamaquoddy Bay.

More difficult, because at once more ambiguous in terms and more vitally important, was the determination of the boundary in the next stage westward from the St. Croix to the St. Lawrence. The British position was a difficult one to maintain. In the days of the struggle with France, Great Britain had tried to push the bounds of the New England colonies as far north as might be, making claims that would hem in France to the barest strip along the south shore of the St. Lawrence. Now that she was heir to the territories and claims of France and had lost her own old colonies, it was somewhat embarrassing, but for diplomats not impossible, to have to urge a line as far south as the urgent needs of the provinces for intercommunication demanded. The letter of the treaty was impossible to interpret with certainty. The phrase, "the Highlands which divide those rivers that empty themselves into the river St. Lawrence from those which fall into the Atlantic Ocean," meant according to the American reading a watershed which was a marshy plateau, and according to the British version a range of hills to the south which involved some keen hairsplitting as to the rivers they divided. The intentions of the parties to the original treaty were probably much as the Americans contended. From the standpoint of neighborly adjustment and the relative need for the land in question, a strong case in equity could be made out for the provinces, which would be cut asunder for all time if a wedge were driven north to the very brink of the St. Lawrence.

As lumbermen and settlers gathered in the border area, the risk of conflict became acute, culminating in the Aroostook War in 1838–39, when the Legislatures of Maine and New Brunswick backed their rival lumberjacks with reckless

jingoism. Diplomacy failed repeatedly to obtain a
compromise line. Arbitration was tried with little
better success, as the United States refused to accept
the award of the King of the Netherlands in 1831.
The diplomats tried once more, and in 1842 Daniel
Webster, the United States Secretary of State, and
Lord Ashburton, the British Commissioner, made a
compromise by which some five thousand miles of
the area in dispute were assigned to Great Britain
and seven thousand to the United States. The
award was not popular on either side, and the public seized eagerly on stories of concealed "Red Line"
maps, stories of Yankee smartness or of British
trickery. Webster, to win the assent of Maine, had
exhibited in the Senate a map found in the French
Archives and very damaging to the American claim.
Later it appeared that the British Government also had found a map equally damaging to its own
claims. The nice question of ethics involved,
whether a nation should bring forward evidence that
would tell against itself, ceased to have more than
an abstract interest when it was demonstrated that
neither map could be considered as one which the
original negotiators had used or marked.[1]

[1] See *The Path of Empire*, by Carl Russell Fish (in *The Chronicles
of America*).

The boundary from the St. Lawrence westward through the Great Lakes and thence to the Lake of the Woods had been laid down in the Treaty of 1783 in the usual vague terms, but it was determined in a series of negotiations from 1794 to 1842 with less friction and heat than the eastern line had caused. From the Lake of the Woods to the Rockies a new line, the forty-ninth parallel, was agreed upon in 1818. Then, as the Pacific Ocean was neared, the difficulties once more increased. There were no treaties between the two countries to limit claims beyond the Rockies. Discovery and settlement, and the rights inherited from or admitted by the Spaniards to the south and by the Russians to the north, were the grounds put forward. British and Canadian fur traders had been the pioneers in overland discovery, but early in the forties thousands of American settlers poured into the Columbia Valley and strengthened the practical case for their country. "Fifty-four forty or fight" — in other words, the calm proposal to claim the whole coast between Mexico and Alaska — became the popular cry in the United States; but in face of the firm attitude of Great Britain and impending hostilities with Mexico, more moderate counsels ruled. Great Britain held out for the Columbia River as the dividing line, and the United States for the forty-ninth parallel throughout. Finally, in 1846, the latter contention was accepted, with a modification to leave Vancouver Island wholly British territory. A postscript to this settlement was added in 1872, when the German Emperor as arbitrator approved the American claim to the island of San Juan in the channel between Vancouver Island and the mainland.[1]

With the most troublesome boundary questions out of the way, it became possible to discuss calmly closer trade relations between the Provinces and the United States. The movement for reciprocal lowering of the tariffs which hampered trade made rapid headway in the Provinces in the late forties and early fifties. British North America was passing out of the pioneer, self-sufficient stage, and now had a surplus to export as well as town-bred needs to be supplied by imports. The spread of settlement and the building of canals and railways brought closer contact with the people to the south. The loss of special privileges in the English market made the United States market more desired. In official circles reciprocity was sought

[1] See *The Path of Empire.*

as a homeopathic cure for the desire for annexation. William Hamilton Merritt, a Niagara border business man and the most persistent advocate of closer trade relations, met little difficulty in securing almost unanimous backing in Canada, while the Maritime Provinces lent their support.

It was more difficult to win over the United States. There the people showed the usual indifference of a big and prosperous country to the needs or opportunities of a small and backward neighbor. The division of power between President and Congress made it difficult to carry any negotiation through to success. Yet these obstacles were overcome. The depletion of the fisheries along the Atlantic coast of the United States made it worth while, as I. D. Andrews, a United States consul in New Brunswick, urged persistently, to gain access to the richer grounds to the north and, if necessary, to offer trade concessions in exchange. At Washington, the South was in the saddle. Its sympathies were strongly for freer trade, but this alone would not have counted had not the advocates of reciprocity convinced the Democratic leaders of the bearing of their policy on the then absorbing issue of slavery. If reciprocity were not arranged, the argument ran, annexation would be sure to come and that would mean the addition to the Union of a group of free-soil States which would definitely tilt the balance against slavery for all time. With the ground thus prepared, Lord Elgin succeeded by adroit and capable diplomacy in winning over the leaders of Congress as well as the Executive to his proposals. The Reciprocity Treaty was passed by the Senate in August, 1854, and by the Legislatures of the United Kingdom, Canada, Prince Edward Island, New Brunswick, and Nova Scotia in the next few months, and of Newfoundland in 1855. This treaty provided for free admission into each country of practically all the products of the farm, forest, mine, and fishery, threw open the Atlantic fisheries, and gave American vessels the use of the St. Lawrence and Canadian vessels the use of Lake Michigan. The agreement was to last for ten years and indefinitely thereafter, subject to termination on one year's notice by either party.

To both countries reciprocity brought undoubted good. Trade doubled and trebled. Each country gained by free access to the nearest sources of supply. The same goods figured largely in the traffic in both directions, the United States importing grain and flour from Canada and exporting it to the Maritime Provinces. In short the benefits which had come to the United States from free and unfettered trade throughout half a continent were now extended to practically a whole continent.

Yet criticism of the new economic régime was not lacking. The growth of protectionist feeling in both countries after 1857 brought about incidents and created an atmosphere which were dangerous to the continuance of close trade relations. In 1858 and 1859 the Canadian Government raised substantially the duties on manufactured goods in order to meet the bills for its lavish railway policy. This increase hit American manufacturers and led to loud complaints that the spirit of the Reciprocity Treaty had been violated. Alexander T. Galt, Canadian Minister of Finance, had no difficulty in showing that the tariff increases were the only feasible sources of revenue, that the agreement with the United States did not cover manufactures, and that the United States itself, faced by war demands and no longer controlled by free trade Southerners, had raised duties still higher. The exports of the United States to the Provinces in the reciprocity period were greater, contrary to the later traditions, than the imports. On economic grounds the case for the continuance of the reciprocity agreement was strong, and probably the treaty would have remained in force indefinitely had not the political passions roused by the Civil War made sanity and neighborliness in trade difficult to maintain.

When the Civil War broke out, the sympathies of Canadians were overwhelmingly on the side of the North. The railway and freer trade had been bringing the two peoples closer together, and time was healing old sores. Slavery was held to be the real issue, and on that issue there were scarcely two opinions in the British Provinces.

Yet in a few months sympathy had given way to angry and suspicious bickering, and the possibility of invasion of Canada by the Northern forces was vigorously debated. This sudden shift of opinion and the danger in which it involved the provinces were both incidents in the quarrel which sprang up between the United States and Great Britain. In Britain as in Canada, opinion, so far as it found open expression, was at first not unfriendly to the North. Then came the anger of the North at Great Britain's legitimate and necessary, though perhaps precipitate, action in acknowledging the South as a belligerent. This action ran counter to the official Northern theory that the revolt of the Southern States was a local riot, of merely domestic concern, and was held to foreshadow a recognition of the independence of the Confederacy. The angry taunts were soon returned. The ruling classes in Great Britain made the discovery that the war was a struggle between chivalrous gentlemen and mercenary counterhoppers and cherished the hope that the failure of the North would discredit, the world over, the democracy which was making uncomfortable claims in England itself. The English trading classes resented the shortage of cotton and the high duties which the protectionist North was imposing. With the defeat of the Union forces at Bull Run the prudent hesitancy of aristocrat and merchant in expressing their views disappeared. The responsible statesmen of both countries, especially Lincoln and Lord John Russell, refused to be stampeded, but unfortunately the leading newspapers served them ill. The *Times*, with its constant sneers and its still more irritating patronizing advice, and the New York *Herald*, bragging and blustering in the frank hope of forcing a war with Britain and France which would reunite South and North and subordinate the slavery issue, did more than any other factors to bring the two countries to the verge of war.

In Canada the tendency in some quarters to reflect English opinion, the disappointment in others that the abolition of slavery was not explicitly pledged by the North, and above all resentment against the threats of the *Herald* and its followers, soon cooled the early friendliness. The leading Canadian newspaper, for many years a vigorous opponent of slavery, thus summed up the situation in August, 1861:

The insolent bravado of the Northern press towards Great Britain and the insulting tone assumed toward these Provinces have unquestionably produced a marked change in the feelings of our people. When the war commenced, there was only one feeling, of hearty sympathy with the North, but now it is very different. People have lost sight of the character of the struggle in the exasperation excited by the injustice and abuse showered upon us by the party with which we sympathized.[1]

The *Trent* affair brought matters to a sobering climax.[2] When it was settled, resentment lingered, but the tension was never again so acute. Both in

[1] Toronto *Globe*, August 7, 1861.
[2] See *Abraham Lincoln and the Union*, by Nathaniel W. Stephenson (in *The Chronicles of America*).

Great Britain and in Canada the normal sympathy with the cause of the Union revived as the war went on. In England the classes continued to be pro-Southern in sympathy, but the masses, in spite of cotton famines, held resolutely to their faith in the cause of freedom. After Lincoln's emancipation of the slaves, the view of the English middle classes more and more became the view of the nation. In Canada, pro-Southern sentiment was strong in the same classes and particularly in Montreal and Toronto, where there were to be found many Southern refugees, some of whom made a poor return for hospitality by endeavoring to use Canada as a base for border raids. Yet in the smaller towns and in the country sympathy was decidedly on the other side, particularly after the *Herald* had ceased its campaign of bluster and after Lincoln's proclamation had brought the moral issue again to the fore. The fact that a large number of Canadians, popularly set at forty thousand, enlisted in the Northern armies, is to be explained in part by the call of adventure and the lure of high bounties, but it must also be taken to reflect the sympathy of the mass of the people.

In the United States resentment was slower in passing. While the war was on, prudence forbade

any overt act. When it was over, the bill for the
Alabama raids and the taunts of the *Times* came
in. Great Britain paid in the settlement of the *Alabama* claims.[1] Canada suffered by the abrogation
of the Reciprocity Treaty at the first possible date,
and by the connivance of the American authorities
in the Fenian raids of 1866 and 1870. Yet for
Canada the outcome was by no means ill. If the
Civil War did not bring forth a new nation in the
South, it helped to make one in the far North.
A common danger drew the scattered British
Provinces together and made ready the way for
the coming Dominion of Canada.

It was not from the United States alone that an
impetus came for the closer union of the British
Provinces. The same period and the same events
ripened opinion in the United Kingdom in favor of
some practical means of altering a colonial relationship which had ceased to bring profit but which had
not ceased to be a burden of responsibility and risk.

The British Empire had its beginning in the initiative of private business men, not in any conscious policy of state. Yet as the Empire grew
the teaching of doctrinaires and the example

[1] See *The Day of the Confederacy*, by Nathaniel W. Stephenson; and
The Path of Empire (in *The Chronicles of America*).

of other colonial powers had developed a definite policy whereby the plantations overseas were to be made to serve the needs of the nation at home. The end of empire was commercial profit; the means, the political subordination of the colonies; the debit entry, the cost of the military and naval and diplomatic services borne by the mother country. But the course of events had now broken down this theory. Britain, for her own good, had abandoned protection, and with it fell the system of preference and monopoly in colonial markets. Not only preference had gone but even equality. The colonies, notably Canada, which was most influenced by the United States, were perversely using their new found freedom to protect their own manufacturers against all outsiders, Britain included. When Sheffield cutlers, hard hit by Canada's tariff, protested to the Colonial Secretary and he echoed their remonstrance, the Canadian Minister of Finance, A. T. Galt, stoutly refused to heed. "Self-government would be utterly annihilated," Galt replied in 1860, "if the views of the Imperial Government were to be preferred to those of the people of Canada. It is therefore the duty of the present government distinctly to affirm the right of the Canadian legislature to adjust the taxation of the people in the way they deem best — even if it should unfortunately happen to meet the disapproval of the Imperial Ministry." Clearly, if trade advantage were the chief purpose of empire, the Empire had lost its reason for being.

With the credit entry fading, the debit entry loomed up bigger. Hardly had the Corn Laws been abolished when Radical critics called on the British Government to withdraw the redcoat garrisons from the colonies: no profit, no defense. Slowly but steadily this reduction was effected. To fill the gaps, the colonies began to strengthen their militia forces. In Canada only a beginning had been made in the way of defense when the *Trent* episode brought matters to a crisis. If war broke out between the United States and Great Britain, Canada would be the battlefield. Every Canadian knew it; nothing could be clearer. When the danger of immediate war had passed, the Parliament of Canada turned to the provision of more adequate defense. A bill providing for a compulsory levy was defeated in 1862, more on personal and party grounds than on its own merits, and the Ministry next in office took the other course of increasing the volunteer force and of providing for officers' training. Compared with any earlier arrangements for defense, the new plans marked a great advance; but when judged in the light of the possible necessity of repelling American invasion, they were plainly inadequate. A burst of criticism followed from England; press and politicians joined in denouncing the blind and supine colonials. Did they not know that invasion by the United States was inevitable? "If the people of the North fail," declared a noble lord, "they will attack Canada as a compensation for their losses; if they succeed, they will attack Canada in the drunkenness of victory." If such an invasion came, Britain had neither the power nor the will, the *Times* declared, to protect Canada without any aid on her part; not the power, for "our empire is too vast, our population too small, our antagonist too powerful"; not the will, for "we no longer monopolize the trade of the colonies; we no longer job their patronage." To these amazing attacks Canadians replied that they knew the United States better than Englishmen did. They were prepared to take their share in defense, but they could not forget that if war came it would not be by any act of Canada. It was soon noted that those who most loudly denounced Canada for not arming to the teeth were the Southern sympathizers. "The

Times has done more than its share in creating bad feeling between England and the United States," declared a Toronto newspaper, "and would have liked to see the Canadians take up the quarrel which it has raised. . . . We have no idea of Canada being made a victim of the Jefferson Bricks on either side of the Atlantic."

The question of defense fell into the background when the war ended and the armies of the Union went back to their farms and shops. But the discussion left in the minds of most Englishmen the belief that the possession of such colonies was a doubtful blessing. Manchester men like Bright, Liberals like Gladstone and Cornewall Lewis, Conservatives like Lowe and Disraeli, all came to believe that separation was only a question of time. Yet honor made them hesitate to set the defenseless colonies adrift to be seized by the first hungry neighbor.

At this juncture the plans for uniting all the colonies in one great federation seemed to open a way out; united, the colonies could stand alone. Thus Confederation found support in Britain as well as a stimulus from the United States. This, however, was not enough. Confederation would not have come when it did — and that might have

meant it would never have come at all — had not
party and sectional deadlock forced Canadian
politicians to seek a remedy in a wider union.

At first all had gone well with the Union of 1841.
It did not take the politicians long to learn how to
use the power that responsible government put
into their hands. After Elgin's day the Governor
General fell back into the rôle of constitutional
monarch which cabinet control made easy for him.
In the forties, men had spoken of Sydenham and
Bagot, Metcalfe and Elgin; in the fifties, they
spoke of Baldwin and La Fontaine, Hincks and
Macdonald and Cartier and Brown, and less and
less of the Governors in whose name these men
ruled. Politics then attracted more of the country's ablest men than it does now, and the party
leaders included many who would have made their
mark in any parliament in the world. Baldwin and
La Fontaine, united to the end, resigned office in
1851, believing that they had played their part
in establishing responsible government and feeling
out of touch with the radical elements of their
following who were demanding further change.
Their place was taken in Canada West by Hincks,
an adroit tactician and a skilled financier, intent
on railway building and trade development; and

in Canada East by Morin, a somewhat colorless lieutenant of La Fontaine.

But these leaders in turn soon gave way to new men; and the political parties gradually fell into a state of flux. In Canada West there were still a few Tories, survivors of the Family Compact and last-ditch defenders of privilege in Church and State, a growing number of moderate Conservatives, a larger group of moderate Liberals, and a small but aggressive extreme left wing of "Clear Grits," mainly Scotch Presbyterians, foes of any claim to undue power on the part of class or clergy. In Canada East the English members from the Townships, under A. T. Galt, were ceasing to vote as a unit, and the main body of French-Canadian members were breaking up into a moderate Liberal party, and a smaller group of *Rouges*, fiery young men under the leadership of Papineau, now returned from exile, were crusading against clerical pretensions and all the established order.

The situation was one made to the hand of a master tactician. The time brought forth the man. John A. Macdonald, a young Kingston lawyer of Tory upbringing, or "John A.", as generation after generation affectionately called him, was to prove the greatest leader of men in Canada's annals. Shrewd, tactful, and genial, never forgetting a face or a favor, as popular for his human frailties as for his strength, Macdonald saw that the old party lines drawn in the days of the struggle for responsible government were breaking down and that the future lay with a union of the moderate elements in both parties and both sections. He succeeded in 1854 in bringing together in Canada West a strong Liberal-Conservative group and in effecting a permanent alliance with the main body of French-Canadian Liberals, now under the leadership of Cartier, a vigorous fighter and an easy-going opportunist. With the addition of Galt as the financial expert, these allies held power throughout the greater part of the next dozen years. Their position was not unchallenged. The Clear Grits had found a leader after their own heart in George Brown, a Scotchman of great ability, a hard hitter and a good hater — especially of slavery, the Roman Catholic hierarchy, and "John A." Through his newspaper, the Toronto *Globe*, he wielded a power unique in Canadian journalism. The *Rouges*, now led by A. A. Dorion, a man of stainless honor and essentially moderate temper, withdrew from their extreme anti-clerical position but could not live down their youth or make head against the forces of conservatism in their province. They did not command many votes in the House, but every man of them was an orator, and they remained through all vicissitudes a power to reckon with.

Step by step, under Liberal and under Liberal-Conservative Governments, the programme of Canadian Liberalism was carried into effect. Self-government, at least in domestic affairs, had been attained. An effective system of municipal government and a good beginning in popular education followed. The last link between Church and State was severed in 1854 when the Clergy Reserves were turned over to the municipalities for secular purposes, with life annuities for clergymen who had been receiving stipends from the Reserves. In Lower Canada the remnants of the old feudal system, the rights of the seigneurs, were abolished in the same year with full compensation from the state. An elective upper Chamber took the place of the appointed Legislative Council a year later. The Reformers, as the Clear Grits preferred to call themselves officially, should perhaps have been content with so much progress. They insisted, however, that a new and more intolerable privilege had arisen — the privilege which Canada East held of equal representation in the Legislative Assembly long after its population had fallen behind that of Canada West.

The political union of the two Canadas in fact had never been complete. Throughout the Union period there were two leaders in each Cabinet, two Attorney Generals, and two distinct judicial systems. Every session laws were passed applying to one section alone. This continued separation had its beginning in a clause of the Union Act itself, which provided that each section should have equal representation in the Assembly, even though Lower Canada then had a much larger population than Upper Canada. When the tide of overseas immigration put Canada West well in the lead, it in its turn was denied the full representation its greater population warranted. First the Conservatives, and later the Clear Grits, took up the cry of "Representation by Population." It was not difficult to convince the average Canada West elector that it was an outrage that three French-Canadian voters should count as much as four English-speaking voters. Macdonald, relying for power on his alliance with Cartier, could not accept the demand, and saw seat after seat in Canada West fall to Brown and his "Rep. by Pop."

crusaders. Brown's success only solidified Canada East against him, until, in the early sixties, party lines coincided almost with sectional lines. Parties were so closely matched that the life of a Ministry was short. In the three years ending in 1864 there were two general elections and four Ministries. Political controversy became bitterly personal, and corruption was spreading fast.

Constant efforts were made to avert the threatened deadlock. Macdonald, who always trusted more to personal management than to constitutional expedients, won over one after another of the opponents who troubled him, and thus postponed the day of reckoning. Rival plans of constitutional reform were brought forward. The simplest remedy was the repeal of the union, leaving each province to go its own way. But this solution was felt to be a backward step and one which would create more problems than it would solve. More support was given the double majority principle, a provision that no measure affecting one section should be passed unless a majority from that section favored it, but this method broke down when put to a practical test. The *Rouges*, and later Brown, put forward a plan for the abolition of legislative union in favor of a federal union of the two

Canadas. This lacked the wide vision of the fourth suggestion, which was destined to be adopted as the solution, namely, the federation of all British North America.

Federal union, it was urged, would solve party and sectional deadlock by removing to local legislatures the questions which created the greatest divergence of opinion. The federal union of the Canadas alone or the federal union of all British North America would either achieve this end. But there were other ends in view which only the wider plan could serve. The needs of defense demanded a single control for all the colonies. The probable loss of the open market of the United States made it imperative to unite all the provinces in a single free trade area. The first faint stirrings of national ambition, prompting the younger men to throw off the leading strings of colonial dependence, were stimulated by the vision of a country which would stretch from sea to sea. The westward growth of the United States and the reports of travelers were opening men's eyes to the possibilities of the vast lands under the control of the Hudson's Bay Company and the need of asserting authority over these northern regions if they were to be held for the Crown. Eastward, also, men were awaking to their isolation. There was not, in the Maritime Provinces, any popular desire for union with the Canadas or any political crisis compelling drastic remedy, but the need of union for defense was felt in some quarters, and ambitious politicians who had mastered their local fields were beginning to sigh for larger worlds to conquer.

It took the patient and courageous striving of many men to make this vision of a united country a reality. The roll of the Fathers of Confederation is a long and honored one. Yet on that roll there are some outstanding names, the names of men whose services were not merely devoted but indispensable. The first to bring the question within the field of practical politics was A. T. Galt, but when attempt after attempt in 1864 to organize a Ministry with a safe working majority had failed, it was George Brown who proposed that the party leaders should join hands in devising some form of federation. Macdonald had hitherto been a stout opponent of all change but, once converted, he threw himself into the struggle with energy. He never appeared to better advantage than in the negotiations of the next few years, steering the ship of Confederation through the perilous shoals of personal and sectional jealousies. Few had a harder or a more important task than Cartier's — reconciling Canada East to a project under which it would be swamped, in the proposed federal House, by the representatives of four or five English-speaking provinces. McDougall, a Canada West Reformer, shared with Brown the credit for awakening Canadians to the value of the Far West and to the need of including it in their plans of expansion. D'Arcy McGee, more than any other, fired the imagination of the people with glowing pictures of the greatness and the limitless possibilities of the new nation. Charles Tupper, the head of a Nova Scotia Conservative Ministry which had overthrown the old tribune, Joseph Howe, had the hardest and seemingly most hopeless task of all; for his province appeared to be content with its separate existence and was inflamed against union by Howe's eloquent opposition; but to Tupper a hard fight was as the breath of his nostrils. In New Brunswick, Leonard Tilley, a man of less vigor but equal determination, led the struggle until Confederation was achieved.

It was in June, 1864, that the leaders of the Parliament of Canada became convinced that federation was the only way out. A coalition Cabinet was formed, with Sir Étienne Taché as nominal

Premier, and with Macdonald, Brown, Cartier, and Galt all included. An opening for discussing the wider federation was offered by a meeting which was to be held in Charlottetown, Prince Edward Island, of delegates from the three Maritime Provinces to consider the formation of a local union. There, in September, 1864, went eight of the Canadian Ministers. Their proposals met with favor. A series of banquets brought the plans before the public, seemingly with good results. The conference was resumed a month later at Quebec. Here, in sixteen working days, delegates from Canada, Nova Scotia, New Brunswick, Prince Edward Island, and also from Newfoundland, thirty-three in all, after frank and full deliberation behind closed doors, agreed upon the terms of union. Macdonald's insistence upon a legislative union, wiping out all provincial boundaries, was overridden; but the lesson of the conflict between the federal and state jurisdiction in the United States was seen in provisions to strengthen the central authority. The general government was empowered to appoint the lieutenant governors of the various provinces and to veto any provincial law; to it were assigned all legislative powers not specifically granted to the provinces; and a subsidy granted by the general government in lieu of the customs revenues resigned by the provinces still further increased their dependence upon the central authority.

It had taken less than three weeks to draw up the plan of union. It took nearly three years to secure its adoption. So far as Canada was concerned, little trouble was encountered. British traditions of parliamentary supremacy prevented any direct submission of the question to the people; but their support was clearly manifested in the press and on the platform, and the legislature ratified the project with emphatic majorities from both sections of the province. Though it did not pass without opposition, particularly from the *Rouges* under Dorion and from steadfast supporters of old ways like Christopher Dunkin and Sandfield Macdonald, the fight was only half-hearted. Not so, however, in the provinces by the sea. The delegates who returned from the Quebec Conference were astounded to meet a storm of criticism. Local pride and local prejudice were aroused. The thrifty maritime population feared Canadian extravagance and Canadian high tariffs. They were content to remain as they were and fearful of the unknown. Here and there advocates

of annexation to the United States swelled the
chorus. Merchants in Halifax and St. John feared
that trade would be drawn away to Montreal.
Above all, Howe, whether because of personal
pique or of intense local patriotism, had put himself at the head of the agitation against union,
and his eloquence could still play upon the prejudices of the people. The Tilley Government in
New Brunswick was swept out of power early in
1865. Prince Edward Island and Newfoundland
both drew back, the one for eight years, the other
to remain outside the fold to the present day. In
Nova Scotia a similar fate was averted only by
Tupper's Fabian tactics. Then the tide turned.
In New Brunswick the Fenian Raids, pressure from
the Colonial Office, and the blunders of the anti-
Confederate Government brought Tilley back to
power on a Confederation platform a year later.
Tupper seized the occasion and carried his motion
through the Nova Scotia House. Without seeking
further warrant the delegates from Canada, Nova
Scotia, and New Brunswick met in London late in
1866, and there in consultation with the Colonial
Office drew up the final resolutions. They were
embodied in the British North America Act which
went through the Imperial Parliament not only

without raising questions but even without exciting interest. On July 1, 1867, the Dominion of Canada, as the new federation was to be known, came into being. It is a curious coincidence that the same date witnessed the establishment of the North German Bund, which in less than three years was to expand into the German Empire.

CHAPTER IV

THE DAYS OF TRIAL

THE federation of the four provinces was an excellent achievement, but it was only a beginning on the long, hard road to nationhood. The Fathers of Confederation had set their goal and had proclaimed their faith. It remained for the next generation to seek to make their vision a reality. It was still necessary to make the Dominion actual by bringing in all the lands from sea to sea. And when, on paper, Canada covered half a continent, union had yet to be given body and substance by railway building and continuous settlement. The task of welding two races and many scattered provinces into a single people would call for all the statesmanship and prudence the country had to give. To chart the relations between the federal and the provincial authorities, which had so nearly brought to shipwreck the federal experiment of Canada's great neighbor, was like navigating an unknown sea. And what was to be the attitude of the new Dominion, half nation, half colony, to the mother country and to the republic to the south, no one could yet foretell.

The first problem which faced the Dominion was the organization of the new machinery of government. It was necessary to choose a federal Administration to guide the Parliament which was soon to meet at Ottawa, the capital of the old Canada since 1858 and now accepted as the capital of the larger Canada. It was necessary also to establish provincial Governments in Canada West, henceforth known as Ontario and in Canada East, or Quebec. The provinces of New Brunswick and Nova Scotia were to retain their existing provincial Governments.

There was no doubt as to whom the Governor General, Lord Monck, should call to form the first federal Administration. Macdonald had proved himself easily the greatest leader of men the four provinces had produced. The entrance of two new provinces into the union, with all the possibilities of new party groupings and new personal alliances it involved, created a situation in which he had no rival. His great antagonist, Brown, passed off the parliamentary stage. When he proposed a coalition to carry through federation, Brown had recognized that he was sacrificing his chief political asset, the discontent of Canada West. But he was too true a patriot to hesitate a moment on that score, and in any case he was sufficiently confident of his own abilities to believe that he could hold his own in a fresh field. In this expectation he was deceived. No man among his contemporaries surpassed him in sheer ability, in fearless honesty, in vigor of debate, but he lacked Macdonald's genial and supple art of managing men. And with broad questions of state policy for the moment out of the way, it was capacity in managing men that was to count in determining success. Never afterward did Brown take an active part in parliamentary life, though still a power in the land through his newspaper, the Toronto *Globe*, which was regarded as the Scotch Presbyterian's second Bible. Of the other leaders of old Canada, Cartier with failing health was losing his vigor and losing also the prestige with his party which his solid Canada East majority had given him; Galt soon retired to private business, with occasional incursions into diplomacy; and McGee fell a victim in 1868 to a Fenian assassin. From the Maritime Provinces the ablest recruit was Tupper, the most dogged fighter in Canadian parliamentary annals and a lifelong sworn ally of Macdonald.

It was at first uncertain what the grouping of parties would be. Macdonald naturally wished to retain the coalition which assured him unquestioned mastery, and the popular desire to give Confederation a good start also favored such a course. In his first Cabinet, formed with infinite difficulty, with provinces, parties, religions, races, all to consider in filling a limited number of posts, Macdonald included six Liberal ministers out of thirteen, three from Ontario, and three from the Maritime Provinces. Yet if an Opposition had not existed, it would have been necessary to create one in order to work the parliamentary machine. The attempt to keep the coalition together did not long succeed. On the eve of the first federal election the Ontario Reformers in convention decided to oppose the Government, even though it contained three of their former leaders. In the contest, held in August and September, 1867, Macdonald triumphed in every province except Nova Scotia but faced a growing Opposition party. Under the virtual leadership of Alexander Mackenzie, fragments of parties from the four provinces were

united into a single Liberal group. In a few years
the majority of the Liberal rank and file were back
in the fold, and the Liberal members in the Cabinet
had become frankly Conservative. Coalition had
faded away.

Within six years after Confederation the whole
northern half of the continent had been absorbed by
Canada. The four original provinces comprised
only one-tenth of the area of the present Dominion, some 377,000 square miles as against 3,730,-
000 today. The most easterly of the provinces,
little Prince Edward Island, had drawn back in
1865, content in isolation. Eight years later this
province entered the fold. Hard times and a
glimpse of the financial strength of the new federation had wrought a change of heart. The solution
of the century-old problem of the island, absentee
landlordism, threatened to strain the finances of
the province; and men began to look to Ottawa for
relief. A railway crisis turned their thoughts in
the same direction. The provincial authorities had
recently arranged for the building of a narrow-
gauge road from one end of the island to the other.
It was agreed that the contractors should be paid
£5000 a mile in provincial debentures, but without

any stipulation as to the total length, so that the builders caused the railway to meander and zig-zag freely in search of lower grades or long paying stretches. In 1873, which was everywhere a year of black depression, it was found that these debentures, which were pledged by the contractors to a local bank for advances, could not be sold except at a heavy loss. The directors of the bank were influential in the Government of the province. It was not surprising, therefore, that the government soon opened negotiations with Ottawa. The Dominion authorities offered generous terms, financing the land purchase scheme, and taking over the railway. Some of the islanders made bitter charges, but the Legislature confirmed the agreement, and on July 1, 1873, Prince Edward Island entered Confederation.

While Prince Edward Island was deciding to come in, Nova Scotia was straining every nerve to get out. There was no question that Nova Scotia had been brought into the union against its will. The provincial Legislature in 1866, it is true, backed Tupper. But the people backed Howe, who thereupon went to London to protest against the inclusion of Nova Scotia without consulting the electors, but he was not heeded. The passing

of the Act only redoubled the agitation. In the
provincial election of 1867, the anti-Confederates
carried thirty-six out of thirty-eight seats. In the
federal election Tupper was the only union candidate returned in nineteen seats contested. A
second delegation was sent to London to demand
repeal. Tupper crossed the ocean to counter this
effort and was successful. Then he sought out
Howe, urged that further agitation was useless and
could only bring anarchy or, what both counted
worse, a movement for annexation to the United
States, and pressed him to use his influence to
allay the storm. Howe gave way; unfortunately
for his own fame, he went further and accepted a
seat in the federal Cabinet. Many of his old followers kept up the fight, but others decided to
make a bargain with necessity. Macdonald agreed
to give the province "better terms," and the Dominion assumed a larger part of its debt. The
bitterness aroused by Tupper's high-handed pro-
cedure lingered for many a day; but before the
first Parliament was over, repeal had ceased to
be a practical issue.

Union could never be real so long as leagues of
barren, unbroken wilderness separated the maritime from the central provinces. Free intercourse,

ties of trade, knowledge which would sweep away
prejudice, could not come until a railway had
spanned this wilderness. In the fifties plans had
been made for a main trunk line to run from Halifax to the Detroit River. This ambitious scheme
proved too great for the resources of the separate
provinces, but sections of the road were built in
each province. As a condition of Confederation,
the Dominion Government undertook to fill in
the long gaps. Surveys were begun immediately; and by 1876, under the direction of Sandford
Fleming, an engineer of eminence, the Intercolonial
Railway was completed. It never succeeded in
making ends meet financially, but it did make
ends meet politically. In great measure it achieved
the purpose of national solidification for which it
was mainly designed.

Meanwhile the bounds of the Dominion were
being pushed westward to the Pacific. The old
province of Canada, as the heir of New France,
had vague claims to the western plains, but the
Hudson's Bay Company was in possession. The
Dominion decided to buy out its rights and agreed,
in 1869, to pay the Company £300,000 for the
transfer of its lands and exclusive privileges, the
Company to retain its trading posts and two

sections in every township. So far all went well. But the Canadian Government, new to the tasks of empire and not as efficient in administration as it should have been, overlooked the necessity of consulting the wishes and the prejudices of the men on the spot. It was not merely land and buffalo herds which were being transferred but also sovereignty over a people.

In the valley of the Red River there were some twelve thousand *métis*, or half-breeds, descendants of Indian mothers and French or Scottish fathers. The Dominion authorities intended to give them a large share in their own government but neglected to arrange for a formal conference. The *métis* were left to gather their impression of the character and intentions of the new rulers from indiscreet and sometimes overbearing surveyors and land seekers. In 1869, under the leadership of Louis Riel, the one man of education in the settlement, able but vain and unbalanced, and with the Hudson's Bay officials looking on unconcerned, the *métis* decided to oppose being made "the colony of a colony." The Governor sent out from Ottawa was refused entrance, and a provisional Government under Riel assumed control. The Ottawa authorities first tried persuasion and sent a commission of three,

Donald A. Smith (afterwards Lord Strathcona), Colonel de Salaberry, and Vicar General Thibault. Smith was gradually restoring unity and order, when the act of Riel in shooting Thomas Scott, an Ontario settler and a member of the powerful Orange order, set passions flaring. Mgr. Taché, the Catholic bishop of the diocese, on his return aided in quieting the *métis*. Delegates were sent by the Provisional Government to Ottawa, and, though not officially recognized, they influenced the terms of settlement. An expedition under Colonel Wolseley marched through the wilderness north of Lake Superior only to find that Riel and his lieutenants had fled. By the Manitoba Act the Red River country was admitted to Confederation as a self-governing province, under the name of Manitoba, while the country west to the Rockies was given territorial status. The Indian tribes were handled with tact and justice, but though for the time the danger of armed resistance had passed, the embers of discontent were not wholly quenched.

The extension of Canadian sovereignty beyond the Rockies came about in quieter fashion. After Mackenzie had shown the way, Simon Fraser and David Thompson and other agents of the North-West Company took up the work of exploration and fur trading. With the union of the two rival companies in 1821, the Hudson's Bay Company became the sole authority on the Pacific coast. Settlers straggled in slowly until, in the late fifties, the discovery of rich placer gold on the Fraser and later in the Cariboo brought tens of thousands of miners from Australia and California, only to drift away again almost as quickly when the sands began to fail.

Local governments had been established both in Vancouver Island and on the mainland. They were joined in a single province in 1866. One of the first acts of the new Legislature was to seek consolidation with the Dominion. Inspired by an enthusiastic Englishman, Alfred Waddington, who had dreamed for years of a transcontinental railway, the province stipulated that within ten years Canada should complete a road from the Pacific to a junction with the railways of the East. These terms were considered presumptuous on the part of a little settlement of ten or fifteen thousand whites; but Macdonald had faith in the resources of Canada and in what the morrow would bring forth. The bargain was made; and British Columbia entered the Confederation on July 1, 1871.

East and West were now staked out. Only the

Far North remained outside the bounds of the Dominion and this was soon acquired. In 1879 the British Government transferred to Canada all its rights and claims over the islands in the Arctic Archipelago and all other British territory in North America save Newfoundland and its strip of Labrador. From the Atlantic to the Pacific, and from the forty-ninth parallel to the North Pole, now all was Canadian soil.

Confederation brought new powers and new responsibilities and thrust Canada into the field of foreign affairs. It was with slow and groping steps that the Dominion advanced along this new path. Then — as now — for Canada foreign relations meant first and foremost relations with her great neighbor to the south. The likelihood of war had passed. The need for closer trade relations remained. When the Reciprocity Treaty was brought to an end, on March 17, 1866, Canada at first refrained from raising her tariff walls. "The provinces," as George Brown declared in 1874, "assumed that there were matters existing in 1865–66 to trouble the spirit of American statesmen for the moment, and they waited patiently for the sober second thought which was very long in coming, but in the meantime Canada played a good neighbor's part, and incidentally served her own ends, by continuing to grant the United States most of the privileges which had been given under the treaty — free navigation and free goods, and, subject to a license fee, access to the fisheries.''

It was over these fisheries that friction first developed.[1] Canadian statesmen were determined to prevent poaching on the inshore fisheries, both because poaching was poaching and because they considered the fishery privileges the best makeweight in trade negotiations with the United States. At first American vessels were admitted on payment of a license fee; but when, on the increase of the fee, many vessels tried to fish inshore without permission, the license system was abolished, and in 1870 a fleet of revenue cruisers began to police the coast waters. American fishermen chafed at exclusion from waters they had come to consider almost their own, and there were many cases of seizure and of angry charge and countercharge. President Grant, in his message to Congress in 1870, denounced the policy of the Canadian authorities as arbitrary and provocative. Other issues between the two countries were outstanding

[1] See *The Path of Empire.*

as well. Canada had a claim against the United States for not preventing the Fenian Raids of 1866; and the United States had a much bigger bill against Great Britain for neglect in permitting the escape of the *Alabama*. Some settlement of these disputed matters was necessary; and it was largely through the activities of a Canadian banker and politician, Sir John Rose, that an agreement was reached to submit all the issues to a joint commission.

Macdonald was offered and accepted with misgivings a post as one of the five British Commissioners. He pressed the traditional Canadian policy of offering fishery for trade privileges but found no backing in this or other matters from his British colleagues, and he met only unyielding opposition from the American Commissioners. He fell back, under protest, on a settlement of narrower scope, which permitted reciprocity in navigation and bonding privileges, free admission of Canadian and Newfoundland fish to United States markets and of American fishermen to Canadian and Newfoundland waters, and which provided for a subsidiary commission to fix the amount to be paid by the United States for the surplus advantage thus received. The Fenian

Raids claims were not even considered, and Macdonald was angered by this indifference on the part of his British colleagues. "They seem to have only one thing in their minds," he reported privately to Ottawa, "that is, to go home to England with a treaty in their pocket, settling everything, no matter at what cost to Canada." Yet when the time came for the Canadian Parliament to decide whether to ratify the fishery clauses of the Treaty of Washington in which the conclusions of the commission were embodied, Macdonald, in spite of the unpopularity of the bargain in Canada, urged Parliament "to accept the treaty, accept it with all its imperfections, to accept it for the sake of peace and for the sake of the great Empire of which we form a part." The treaty was ratified in 1871 by all the powers concerned; and the stimulus to the peaceful settlement of international disputes given by the Geneva Tribunal which followed[1] justified the subordination of Canada's specific interests.

A change in party now followed in Canada, but the new Government under Alexander Mackenzie was as fully committed as the Government of Sir John Macdonald to the policy of bartering fishery

[1] See *The Path of Empire.*

for trade advantage.   Canada therefore proposed
that instead of carrying out the provisions for a
money settlement, the whole question should be
reopened.   The Administration at Washington was
sympathetic.   George Brown was appointed along
with the British Ambassador, Sir Edward Thorn-
ton, to open negotiations.   Under Brown's energetic leadership a settlement of all outstanding
issues was drafted in 1874, which permitted freedom of trade in natural and in most manufactured
products for twenty-one years, and settled fishery,
coasting trade, navigation, and minor boundary
issues.   But diplomats proposed, and the United
States Senate disposed.   Protectionist feeling was
strong at Washington, and the currency problem
absorbing, and hence this broad and statesmanlike
essay in neighborliness could not secure an hour's
attention.   This plan having failed, the Canadian
Government fell back on the letter of the treaty.
A Commission which consisted of the Honorable
E. H. Kellogg representing the United States, Sir
Alexander T. Galt representing Canada, and the
Belgian Minister to Washington, M. Delfosse, as
chairman, awarded Canada and Newfoundland
$5,500,000 as the excess value of the fisheries for
the ten years the arrangement was to run.   The

award was denounced in the United States as absurdly excessive; but a sense of honor and the knowledge that millions of dollars from the *Alabama* award were still in the Treasury moved the Senate finally to acquiesce, though only for the ten-year term fixed by treaty. In Canada the award was received with delight as a signal proof that when left to themselves Canadians could hold their own. The prevailing view was well summed up in a letter from Mackenzie to the Canadian representative on the Halifax commission, written shortly before the decision: "I am glad you still have hopes of a fair verdict. I am doubly anxious to have it, first, because we are entitled to it and need the dollars, and, second, because it will be the first Canadian diplomatic triumph, and will justify me in insisting that we know our neighbors and our own business better than any Englishmen."

Mackenzie's insistence that Canada must take a larger share in the control of her foreign affairs was too advanced a stand for many of his more conservative countrymen. For others, he did not go far enough. The early seventies saw the rise of a short-lived movement in favor of Canadian independence. To many independence from England seemed the logical sequel to Confederation; and the rapid expansion of Canadian territory over half a continent stimulated national pride and national self-consciousness Opinion in England regarding Canadian independence was still more outspoken. There imperialism was at its lowest ebb. With scarcely an exception, English politicians, from Bright to Disraeli, were hostile or indifferent to connection with the colonies, which had now ceased to be a trade asset and had clearly become a military liability.

But no concrete problem arose to make the matter a political issue. In England a growing uneasiness over the protectionist policies and the colonial ambitions of her European rivals were soon to revive imperial sentiment. In Canada the ties of affection for the old land, as well as the inertia fostered by long years of colonial dependence, kept the independence movement from spreading far. For the time the rising national spirit found expression in economic rather than political channels. The protectionist movement which a few years later swept all Canada before it owed much of its strength to its claim to be the national policy.

But it was not imperial or foreign relations that dominated public interest in the seventies.

Domestic politics were intensely absorbing and bitterly contested. Within five years there came about two sudden and sweeping reversals of power. Parties and Cabinets which had seemed firmly entrenched were dramatically overthrown by sudden changes in the personal factors and in the issues of the day. In the summer of 1872 the second general election for the Dominion was held. The Opposition had now gained in strength. The Government had ceased to be in any real sense a coalition, and most of the old Liberal rank and file were back in the party camp. They had found a vigorous leader in Alexander Mackenzie.

Mackenzie had come to Canada from Scotland in 1842 as a lad of twenty. He worked at his trade as a stonemason, educated himself by wide reading and constant debating, became a successful contractor and, after Confederation, had proved himself one of the most aggressive and uncompromising champions of Upper Canada Liberalism. In the first Dominion Parliament he tacitly came to be regarded as the leader of all the groups opposed to the Macdonald Administration. He was at the same time active in the Ontario Legislature since, for the first five years of Confederation, no law forbade membership in both federal and provincial Parliaments, and the short sessions of that blessed time made such double service feasible. Here he was aided by two other men of outstanding ability, Edward Blake and Oliver Mowat. Blake, the son of a well-to-do Irishman who had been active in the fight for responsible government, became Premier of Ontario in 1871 but retired in 1872 when a law abolishing dual representation made it necessary for him to choose between Toronta ond Ottawa. His place was taken by Mowat, who for a quarter of a century gave the province thrifty, honest, and conservatively progressive government.

In spite of the growing forces opposed to him Macdonald triumphed once more in the election of 1872. Ontario fell away, but Quebec and the Maritime Provinces stood true. A Conservative majority of thirty or forty seemed to assure Macdonald another five-year lease of power. Yet within a year the Pacific Scandal had driven him from office and overwhelmed him in disgrace.

The Pacific Scandal occurred in connection with the financing of the railway which the Dominion Government had promised British Columbia, when that province entered Confederation in 1871, would be built through to the Pacific coast within ten years. The bargain was good politics but poor business. It was a rash undertaking for a people of three and a half millions, with a national revenue of less than twenty million dollars, to pledge itself to build a railway through the rocky wilderness north of Lake Superior, through the trackless plains and prairies of the middle west, and across the mountain ranges that barred the coast. Yet Macdonald had sufficient faith in the country, in himself, and in the happy accidents of time — a confidence that won him the nickname of "Old Tomorrow" — to give the pledge. Then came the question of ways and means. At first the Government planned to build the road. On second thoughts, however, it decided to follow the example set by the United States in the construction of the Union Pacific and Southern Pacific, and to entrust the work to a private company liberally subsidized with land and cash. Two companies were organized with a view to securing the contract, one a Montreal company under Sir Hugh Allan, the foremost Canadian man of business and the head of the Allan steamship fleet, and the other a Toronto company under D. L. Macpherson, who had been concerned in the building of the Grand Trunk. Their rivalry was intense. After the election of

1872 a strong compromise company was formed, with Allan at the head, and to this company the contract was awarded.

When Parliament met in 1872, a Liberal member, L. S. Huntington, made the charge that Allan had really been acting on behalf of certain American capitalists and that he had made lavish contributions to the Government campaign fund in the recent election. In the course of the summer these charges were fully substantiated. Allan was proved by his own correspondence, stolen from his solicitor's office, to have spent over $350,000, largely advanced by his American allies, in buying the favor of newspapers and politicians. Nearly half of this amount had been contributed to the Conservative campaign fund, with the knowledge and at the instance of Cartier and Macdonald. Macdonald, while unable to disprove the charges, urged that there was no connection between the contributions and the granting of the charter. But his defense was not heeded. A wave of indignation swept the country; his own supporters in Parliament fell away; and in November, 1873, he resigned. Mackenzie, who was summoned to form a new Ministry, dissolved Parliament and was sustained by a majority of two to one.

Mackenzie gave the country honest and efficient administration. Among his most important achievements were the reform of elections by the introduction of the secret ballot and the requirement that elections should be held on a single day instead of being spread over weeks, a measure of local option in controlling the liquor traffic, and the establishment of a Canadian Supreme Court and the Royal Military College — the Canadian West Point. But fate and his own limitations were against him. He was too absorbed in the details of administration to have time for the work of a party leader. In his policy of constructing the Canadian Pacific as a government road, after Allan had resigned his charter, he manifested a caution and a slowness that brought British Columbia to the verge of secession. But it was chiefly the world-wide depression that began in his first year of office, 1873, which proved his undoing. Trade was stagnant, bankruptcies multiplied, and acute suffering occurred among the poor in the larger cities. Mackenzie had no solution to offer except patience and economy; and the Opposition were freer to frame an enticing policy. The country was turning toward a high tariff as the solution of its ills. Protection had not hitherto been a party issue in Canada, and it was still uncertain which party would take it up. Finally Mackenzie, who was an ardent free trader, and the Nova Scotia wing of his party triumphed over the protectionists in their own ranks and made a low tariff the party platform. Macdonald, who had been prepared to take up free trade if Mackenzie adopted protection, now boldly urged the high tariff panacea. The promise of work and wages for all, the appeal to national spirit made by the arguments of self-sufficiency and fully rounded development, the desire to retaliate against the United States, which was still deaf to any plea for more liberal trade relations, swept the country. The Conservative minority of over sixty was converted into a still greater majority in the general election of 1878, and the leader whom all men five years before had considered doomed, returned to power, never to lose it while life lasted.

The first task of the new Government, in which Tupper was Macdonald's chief supporter, was to carry out its high tariff pledges. "Tell us how much protection you want, gentlemen," said Macdonald to a group of Ontario manufacturers, "and we'll give you what you need." In the new tariff needs were rated almost as high as wants. Particularly on textiles, sugar, and iron and steel products, duties were raised far beyond the old levels and stimulated investment just as the world-wide depression which had lasted since 1873 passed away. Canada shared in the recovery and gave the credit to the well-advertised political patent medicine taken just before the turn for the better came. For years the National Policy or "N. P.," as its supporters termed it, had all the vogue of a popular tonic.

The next task of the Government was to carry through in earnest the building of the railway to the Pacific. For over a year Macdonald persisted in Mackenzie's policy of government construction but with the same slow and unsatisfactory results. Then an opportunity came to enlist the services of a private syndicate. Four Canadians, Donald A. Smith, a former Hudson's Bay Company factor, George Stephen, a leading merchant and banker of Montreal, James J. Hill and Norman W. Kittson, owners of a small line of boats on the Red River, had joined forces to revive a bankrupt Minnesota railway.[1] They had succeeded beyond all parallel, and the reconstructed road, which later developed into the Great Northern, made them all rich

[1] See *The Railroad Builders*, by John Moody (in *The Chronicles of America*).

overnight. This success whetted their appetite for further western railway building and further millions of rich western acres in subsidies. They met Macdonald and Tupper half way. By the bargain completed in 1881 the Canadian Pacific Railway Company undertook to build and operate the road from the Ottawa Valley to the Pacific coast, in return for the gift of the completed portions of the road (on which the Government spent over $37,000,000), a subsidy of $25,000,000 in cash, 25,000,000 selected acres of prairie land, exemption from taxes, exemption from regulation of rates until ten per cent was earned, and a promise on the part of the Dominion to charter no western lines connecting with the United States for twenty years. The terms were lavish and were fiercely denounced by the Opposition, now under the leadership of Edward Blake. But the people were too eager for railway expansion to criticize the terms. The Government was returned to power in 1882 and the contract held.

The new company was rich in potential resources but weak in available cash. Neither in New York nor in London could purse strings be loosened for the purpose of building a road through what the world considered a barren and Arctic wilderness. But in the faith and vision of the president, George Stephen, and the ruthless energy of the general manager, William Van Horne, American born and trained, the Canadian Pacific had priceless assets. Aided in critical times by further government loans, they carried the project through, and by 1886, five years before the time fixed by their contract, trains were running from Montreal to Port Moody, opposite Vancouver.

A sudden burst of prosperity followed the building of the road. Settlers poured into the West by tens of thousands, eastern investors promoted colonization companies, land values soared, and speculation gave a fillip to every line of trade. The middle eighties were years of achievement, of prosperity, and of confident hope. Then prosperity fled as quickly as it had come. The West failed to hold its settlers. Farm and factory found neither markets nor profits. The country was bled white by emigration. Parliamentary contest and racial feud threatened the hard-won unity. Canada was passing through its darkest hours.

During this period, political friction was incessant. Canada was striving to solve in the eighties the difficult question which besets all federations — the limits between federal and provincial power. Ontario was the chief champion of provincial rights. The struggle was intensified by the fact that a Liberal Government reigned at Toronto and a Conservative Government at Ottawa, as well as by the keen personal rivalry between Mowat and Macdonald. In nearly every constitutional duel Mowat triumphed. The accepted range of the legislative power of the provinces was widened by the decisions of the courts, particularly of the highest court of appeal, the Judicial Committee of the Privy Council in England. The successful resistance of Ontario and Manitoba to Macdonald's attempt to disallow provincial laws proved this power, though conferred by the Constitution, to be an unwieldy weapon. By the middle nineties the veto had been virtually abandoned.

More serious than these political differences was the racial feud that followed the second Riel Rebellion. For a second time the Canadian Government failed to show the foresight and the sympathy required in dealing with an isolated and backward people. The valley of the Saskatchewan, far northwest of the Red River, was the scene of the new difficulty. Here thousands of *métis*, or French half-breeds, had settled. The passing of the buffalo, which had been their chief subsistence, and the arrival of settlers from the East caused them intense alarm. They pressed the Government for certain grants of land and for the retention of the old French custom of surveying the land along the river front in deep narrow strips, rather than according to the chessboard pattern taken over by Canada from the United States. Red tape, indifference, procrastination, rather than any ill-will, delayed the redress of the grievances of the half-breeds. In despair they called Louis Riel back from his exile in Montana. With his arrival the agitation acquired a new and dangerous force. Claiming to be the prophet of a new religion, he put himself at the head of his people and, in the spring of 1885, raised the flag of revolt. His military adviser, Gabriel Dumont, an old buffalo hunter, was a natural-born general, and the half-breeds were good shots and brave fighters. An expedition of Canadian volunteers was rushed west, and the rebellion was put down quickly, but not without some hard fighting and gallant strokes and counterstrokes.

The racial passions roused by this conflict, however, did not pass so quickly. The fate to be meted out to Riel was the burning question. Ontario saw in him the murderer of Scott and an ambitious plotter who had twice stirred up armed rebellion. Quebec saw in him a man of French blood, persecuted because he had stood up manfully for the undoubted rights of his kinsmen. Today experts agree that Riel was insane and should have been spared the gallows on this if on no other account. But at the moment the plea of insanity was rejected. The Government made up for its laxity before the rebellion by severity after it; and in November, 1885, Riel was sent to the scaffold. Bitterness rankled in many a French-Canadian heart for long years after; and in Ontario, where the Orange order was strongly entrenched, a faction threatened "to smash Confederation into its original fragments" rather than submit to "French domination."

Racial and religious passions, once aroused, soon found new fuel to feed upon. Honoré Mercier, a brilliant but unscrupulous leader who had ridden to power in the province of Quebec on the Riel issue, roused Protestant ire by restoring estates which had been confiscated at the conquest in 1763 to the Jesuits and other Roman Catholic authorities, in proportions which the act provided were to be determined by "Our Holy Father the Pope."

In Ontario restrictions began to be imposed on the freedom of French-Canadian communities on the border to make French the sole or dominant tongue in the schoolroom. A little later the controversy was echoed in Manitoba in the repeal by a determined Protestant majority of the denominational school privileges hitherto enjoyed by the Roman Catholic minority.

Economic discontent was widespread. It was a time of low and falling prices. Farmers found the American market barred, the British market flooded, the home market stagnant. The factories stimulated by the "N. P." lacked the growing market they had hoped for. In the West climatic conditions not yet understood, the monopoly of the Canadian Pacific, and the competition of the States to the south, which still had millions of acres of free land, brought settlement to a standstill. From all parts of Canada the "exodus" to the United States continued until by 1890 there were in that country more than one-third as many people of Canadian birth or descent as in Canada itself.

It was not surprising that in these extremities men were prepared to make trial of drastic remedies. Nor was it surprising that it was beyond the

borders of Canada itself that they sought the unity
and the prosperity they had not found at home.
Many looked to Washington, some for unrestricted
trade, a few for political union. Others looked to
London, hoping for a revival of the old imperial
tariff preferences or for some closer political union
which would bring commercial advantages in its
train.

The decade from 1885 to 1895 stands out in the
record of the relations of the English-speaking
peoples as a time of constant friction, of petty
pin pricks, of bluster and retaliation. The United
States was not in a neighborly mood. The memories of 1776, of 1812, and of 1861 had been kept
green by exuberant comment in school textbooks
and by "spread-eagle" oratory. The absence of
any other rivalry concentrated American opposition on Great Britain, and isolation from Old
World interests encouraged a provincial lack of
responsibility. The sins of England in Ireland had
been kept to the fore by the agitation of Parnell
and Davitt and Dillon; and the failure of Home
Rule measures, twice in this decade, stirred Irish-
American antagonism. The accession to power of
Lord Salisbury, reputed to hold the United States
in contempt, and later the foolish indiscretion of

Sir Lionel Sackville-West, British Ambassador at Washington, in intervening in a guileless way in the presidential election of 1888, did as much to nourish ill-will in the United States as the dominance of Blaine and other politicians who cultivated the gentle art of twisting the tail of the British lion.

Protection, with the attitude of economic warfare which it involved and bred, was then at its height. Much of this hostility was directed against Canada, as the nearest British territory. The Dominion, on its part, while persistently seeking closer trade relations, sometimes sought this end in unwise ways. Many good people in Canada were still fighting the War of 1812. The desire to use the inshore fishery privileges as a lever to force tariff reductions led to a rigid and literal enforcement of Canadian rights and claims which provoked widespread anger in New England. The policy of discrimination in canal tolls in favor of Canadian as against United States ports was none the less irritating because it was a retort in kind. And when United States customs officials levied a tax on the tin cans containing fish free by treaty, Canadian officials had retaliated by taxing the baskets containing duty-free peaches.

The most important specific issue was once more

the northeastern fisheries. As a result of notice given by the United States the fisheries clauses of the Treaty of Washington ceased to operate on July 1, 1885. Canada, for the sake of peace, admitted American fishing vessels for the rest of that season, though Canadian fish at once became dutiable. No further grace was given. The Canadian authorities rigidly enforced the rules barring inshore fishing, and in addition denied port privileges to deep-sea fishing vessels and forbade American boats to enter Canadian ports for the purpose of trans-shipping crews, purchasing bait, or shipping fish in bond to the United States. Every time a Canadian fishery cruiser and a Gloucester skipper had a difference of opinion as to the exact whereabouts of the three-mile limit, the press of both countries echoed the conflict. Congress in 1887 empowered the President to retaliate by excluding Canadian vessels and goods from American ports. Happily this power was not used. Cleveland and Secretary of State Bayard were genuinely anxious to have the issue settled. A joint commission drew up a well-considered plan, but in the face of a presidential election the Senate gave it short shrift. Fortunately, however, a *modus vivendi* was arranged by which American vessels were admitted to port privileges on payment of a license. Healing time, a healthful lack of publicity, changing fishing methods, and Canada's abandonment of her old policy of using fishing privileges as a makeweight, gradually eased the friction.

Yet if it was not the fishing question, there was sure to be some other issue — bonding privileges, Canadian Pacific interloping in western rail hauls, tariff rates, or canal tolls — to disturb the peace. Why not seek a remedy once for all, men now began to ask, by ending the unnatural separation between the halves of the continent which God and geography had joined and history and perverse politicians had kept asunder?

The political union of Canada and the United States has always found advocates. In the United States a large proportion, perhaps a majority, of the people have until recently considered that the absorption of Canada into the Republic was its manifest destiny, though there has been little concerted effort to hasten fate. In Canada such course of action has found much less backing. United Empire Loyalist traditions, the ties with Britain constantly renewed by immigration, the dim stirrings of national sentiment, resentment against the trade policy of the United States, have all helped to turn popular sentiment into other channels. Only at two periods, in 1849, and forty years later, has there been any active movement for annexation.

In the late eighties, as in the late forties, commercial depression and racial strife prepared the soil for the seed of annexation. The chief sower in the later period was a brilliant Oxford don, Goldwin Smith, whose sympathy with the cause of the North had brought him to the United States. In 1871, after a brief residence at Cornell, he made his home in Toronto, with high hopes of stimulating the intellectual life and molding the political future of the colony. He so far forsook the strait "Manchester School" of his upbringing as to support Macdonald's campaign for protection in 1878. But that was the limit of his adaptability. To the end he remained out of touch with Canadian feeling. His campaign for annexation, or for the reunion of the English-speaking peoples on this continent, as he preferred to call it, was able and persistent but moved only a narrow circle of readers. It was in vain that he offered the example of Scotland's prosperity after her union with her southern neighbor, or insisted that Canada was cut into four distinct and unrelated sections each of which could find its natural complement only in the territory to the south. Here and there an editor or a minor politician lent some support to his views, but the great mass of the people strongly condemned the movement. There was to be no going back to the parting of the ways: the continent north of Mexico was henceforth to witness two experiments in democracy, not one unwieldy venture.

Commercial union was a half-way measure which found more favor. A North American customs union had been supported by such public men as Stephen A. Douglas, Horace Greeley, and William H. Seward, by official investigators such as Taylor, Derby, and Larned, and by committees of the House of Representatives in 1862, 1876, 1880, and 1884. In Canada it had been endorsed before Confederation by Isaac Buchanan, the father of the protection movement, and by Luther Holton and John Young. Now for the first time it became a practical question. Erastus Wiman, a Canadian who had found fortune in the United States, began in 1887 a vigorous campaign in its favor both in Congress and among the Canadian public. Goldwin Smith lent his dubious aid, leading Toronto and Montreal newspapers joined the movement,

and Ontario farmers' organizations swung to its
support. But the agitation proved abortive owing
to the triumph of high protection in the presidential election of 1888; and in Canada the red herring
of the Jesuits' Estates controversy was drawn
across the trail.

Yet the question would not down. The political
parties were compelled to define their attitude.
The Liberals had been defeated once more in the
election of 1887, where the continuance of the National Policy and of aid to the Canadian Pacific
had been the issue. Their leader, Edward Blake,
had retired disheartened. His place had been taken by a young Quebec lieutenant, Wilfrid Laurier,
who had won fame by his courageous resistance
to clerical aggression in his own province and by
his indictment of the Macdonald Government in
the Riel issue. A veteran Ontario Liberal, Sir
Richard Cartwright, urged the adoption of commercial union as the party policy. Laurier would
not go so far, and the policy of unrestricted reciprocity was made the official programme in 1888.
Commercial union had involved not only absolute
free trade between Canada and the United States
but common excise rates, a common tariff against
the rest of the world, and the division of customs

and excise revenues in some agreed proportion. Unrestricted reciprocity would mean free trade between the two countries, but with each left free to levy what rates it pleased on the products of other countries.

When in 1891 the time came round once more for a general election, it was apparent that reciprocity in some form would be the dominant issue. Though the Republicans were in power in the United States and though they had more than fulfilled their high tariff pledges in the McKinley Act, which hit Canadian farm products particularly hard, there was some chance of terms being made. Reciprocity, as a form of tariff bargaining, really fits in better with protection than with free trade, and Blaine, Harrison's Secretary of State, was committed to a policy of trade treaties and trade bargaining. In Canada the demand for the United States market had grown with increasing depression. The Liberals, with their policy of unrestricted reciprocity, seemed destined to reap the advantage of this rising tide of feeling. Then suddenly, on the eve of the election, Sir John Macdonald sought to cut the ground from under the feet of his opponents by the announcement that in the course of a discussion of Newfoundland matters the United States had taken the initiative in suggesting to Canada a settlement of all outstanding difficulties, fisheries, coasting trade, and tariffs, on the basis of a renewal and extension of the Reciprocity Treaty of 1854.   This policy promised to meet all legitimate economic needs of the country and at the same time avoid the political dangers of the more sweeping policy.   Its force was somewhat weakened by the denials of Secretary Blaine that he had taken the initiative or made any definite promises. As the election drew near and revelations of the annexationist aims of some supporters of the wider trade policy were made, the Government made the loyalty cry its strong card. "The old man, the old flag, and the old policy," saved the day. In Ontario and Quebec the two parties were evenly divided, but the West and the Maritime Provinces, the "shreds and patches of Confederation," as Sir Richard Cartwright, too ironic and vitriolic in his speech for political success, termed them, gave the Government a working majority, which was increased in by-elections.

Again in power, the Government made a formal attempt to carry out its pledges.   Two pilgrimages were made to Washington, but the negotiators were too far apart to come to terms. With the triumph of the Democrats in 1892 and the lowering of the tariff on farm products which followed, there came a temporary improvement in trade relations. But the tariff reaction and the silver issue brought back the Republicans and led to that climax in agricultural protection, the Dingley Act of 1897, which killed among Canadians all reciprocity longings and compelled them to look to themselves for salvation. Although Canadians were anxious for trade relations, they were not willing to be bludgeoned into accepting one-sided terms. The settlement of the Bering Sea dispute in 1893 by a board of arbitration, which ruled against the claims of the United States but suggested a restriction of pelagic sealing by agreement, removed one source of friction. Hardly was that out of the way when Cleveland's Venezuela message brought Great Britain and the United States once more to the verge of war. In such a war Canadians knew they would be the chief sufferers, but in 1895, as in 1862, they did not flinch and stood ready to support the mother country in any outcome. The Venezuela episode stirred Canadian feeling deeply, revived interest in imperialism, and ended the last lingering remnants of any sentiment for annexation.

As King Edward I was termed "the hammer of the Scots," so McKinley and Cleveland became "the hammer of the Canadians," welding them into unity.

While most Canadians were ceasing to look to Washington for relief, an increasing number were looking once more to London. The revival of imperial sentiment which began in the early eighties, seemed to promise new and greater possibilities for the colonies overseas. Political union in the form of imperial federation and commercial union through reciprocal tariff preferences were urged in turn as the cure for all Canada's ills. Neither solution was adopted. The movement greatly influenced the actual trend of affairs, but there was to be no mere turning back to the days of the old empire.

The period of *laissez faire* in imperial matters, of Little Englandism, drew to a close in the early eighties. Once more men began to value empire, to seek to annex new territory overseas, and to bind closer the existing possessions. The world was passing through a reaction destined to lead to the earth-shaking catastrophe of 1914. The ideals of peace and free trade preached and to some

degree practiced in the fifties and sixties were
passing under an eclipse. In Europe the swing to
free trade had halted, and nation after nation was
becoming aggressively protectionist. The triumph
of Prussia in the War of 1870 revived and intensified military rivalry and military preparations
on the part of all the powers of Europe. A new
scramble for colonies and possessions overseas began, with the late comers nervously eager to make
up for time lost. In this reaction Britain shared.
Protection raised its head again in England; only
by tariffs and tariff bargaining, the Fair Traders
insisted, could the country hold its own. Odds
and ends of territory overseas were annexed and
a new value was attached to the existing colonies.
The possibility of obtaining from them military
support and trade privileges, the desirability of re-
turning to the old ideal of a self-contained and centralized empire, appealed now to influential groups.
This goal might be attained by different paths.
From the United Kingdom came the policy of imperial federation and from the colonies the policy
of preferential trade as means to this end.

In 1884 the Imperial Federation League was
organized in London with important men of both
parties in its ranks. It urged the setting up in

London of a new Parliament, in which the United Kingdom and all the colonies where white men predominated would be represented according to population. This Parliament would have power to frame policies, to make laws, and to levy taxes for the whole Empire. To the colonist it offered an opportunity to share in the control of foreign affairs; to the Englishman it offered the support of colonies fast growing to power and the assurance of one harmonious policy for all the Empire. Both in Britain and overseas the movement received wide support and seemed for a time likely to sweep all before it. Then a halt came.

Imperial federation had been brought forward a generation too late to succeed. The Empire had been developing upon lines which could not be made to conform to the plans for centralized parliamentary control. It was not possible to go back to the parting of the ways. Slowly, unconsciously, unevenly, yet steadily, the colonies had been ceasing to be dependencies and had been becoming nations. With Canada in the vanguard they had been taking over one power after another which had formerly been wielded by the Government of the United Kingdom. It was not likely that they would relinquish these powers or that self-governing colonies would consent to be subordinated to a Parliament in London in which each would have only a fragmentary representation.

The policy of imperial coöperation which began to take shape during this period sought to reconcile the existing desire for continuing the connection with the mother country with the growing sense of national independence. This policy involved two different courses of action: first, the colonies must assert and secure complete self-government on terms of equality with the United Kingdom; second, they must unite as partners or allies in carrying out common tasks and policies and in building up machinery for mutual consultation and harmonious action.

It was chiefly in matters of trade and tariffs that progress was made in the direction of self-government. Galt had asserted in 1859 Canada's right to make her own tariffs, and Macdonald twenty years later had carried still further the policy of levying duties upon English as well as foreign goods. That economic point was therefore settled, but it was a slower matter to secure control of treaty-making powers. When Galt and Huntington urged this right in 1871 and when Blake and Mackenzie pressed it ten years later, Macdonald opposed such a demand as equivalent to an effort for independence. Yet he himself was compelled to change his conservative attitude. After 1877 Canada ceased to be bound by commercial treaties made by the United Kingdom, unless it expressly desired to be included. In 1879 Galt was sent to Europe to negotiate Canadian trade agreements with France and Spain; and in the next decade Tupper carried negotiations with France to a successful conclusion, though the treaty was formally concluded between France and Britain. By 1891 the Canadian Parliament could assert with truth that "the self-governing colonies are recognized as possessing the right to define their respective fiscal relations to all countries." But Canada as yet took no step toward assuming a share in her own naval defense, though the Australasian colonies made a beginning, along colonial rather than national lines, by making a money contribution to the British navy.

The second task confronting the policy of imperial coöperation was a harder one. For a partnership between colony and mother country there were no precedents. Centralized empires there had been; colonies there had been which had grown into independent states; but there was no instance of an empire ceasing to be an empire, of colonies

becoming self-governing states and then turning
to closer and coöperative union with one another
and with the mother country.

Along this unblazed trail two important advances were made. The initiative in the first came
from Canada. In 1880 a High Commissioner was
appointed to represent Canada in London. The
appointment of Sir Alexander Galt and the policy
which it involved were significant. The Governor-
General had ceased to be a real power; he was becoming the representative not of the British Government but of the King; and, like the King, he
governed by the advice of the responsible ministers in the land where he resided. His place as
the link between the Government of Canada and
the Government of Britain was now taken in part
by the High Commissioner. The relationship of
Canada to the United Kingdom was becoming one
of equality not of subordination.

The initiative in the second step came from
Britain, though Canada's leaders gave the movement its final direction. Imperial federationists
urged Lord Salisbury to summon a conference of
the colonies to discuss the question they had at
heart. Salisbury doubted the wisdom of such a
policy but agreed in 1887 to call a conference to

discuss matters of trade and defense. Every self-governing colony sent representatives to this first Colonial Conference; but little immediate fruit came of its sessions. In 1894 a second Conference was held at Ottawa, mainly to discuss intercolonial preferential trade. Only a beginning had been made, but already the Conferences were coming to be regarded as meetings of independent governments and not, as the federationists had hoped, the germ of a single dominating new government. The Imperial Federation League began to realize that it was making little progress and dissolved in 1893.

Preferential trade was the alternative path to imperial federation. Macdonald had urged it in 1879 when he found British resentment strong against his new tariff. Again, ten years later, when reciprocity with the United States was finding favor in Canada, imperialists urged the counter-claims of a policy of imperial reciprocity, of special tariff privileges to other parts of the Empire. The stumblingblock in the way of such a policy was England's adherence to free trade. For the protectionist colonies preference would mean only a reduction of an existing tariff. For the United Kingdom, however, it would mean a complete

reversal of fiscal policy and the abandonment of free
trade for protection in order to make discrimination possible. Few Englishmen believed such a
reversal possible, though every trade depression revived talk of "fair trade" or tariffs for bargaining
purposes. A further obstacle to preferential trade
lay in the existence of treaties with Belgium and
Germany, concluded in the sixties, assuring them
all tariff privileges granted by any British colony
to Great Britain or to sister colonies. In 1892 the
Liberal Opposition in Canada indicated the line
upon which action was eventually to be taken by
urging a resolution in favor of granting an immediate and unconditional preference on British goods
as a step toward freer trade and in the interest of
the Canadian consumer.

Little came of looking either to London or to
Washington. Until the middle nineties Canada
remained commercially stagnant and politically
distracted. Then came a change of heart and a
change of policy. The Dominion realized at last
that it must work out its own salvation.

In March, 1891, Sir John Macdonald was returned to office for the sixth time since Confederation, but he was not destined to enjoy power long.
The winter campaign had been too much for his

weakened constitution, and he died on June 6, 1891. No man had been more hated by his political opponents, no man more loved by his political followers. Today the hatred has long since died, and the memory of Sir John Macdonald has become the common pride of Canadians of every party, race, and creed. He had done much to lower the level of Canadian politics; but this fault was forgiven when men remembered his unfailing courage and confidence, his constructive vision and fertility of resource, his deep and unquestioned devotion to his country.

The Conservative party had with difficulty survived the last election. Deprived of the leader who for so long had been half its force, the party could not long delay its break-up. No one could be found to fill Macdonald's place. The helm was taken in turn by J. J. C. Abbott, "the confidential family lawyer of the party," by Sir John Thompson, solid and efficient though lacking in imagination, and by Sir Mackenzie Bowell, an Ontario veteran. Abbott was forced to resign because of ill health; Thompson died in office; and Bowell was forced out by a revolt within the party. Sir Charles Tupper, then High Commissioner in London, was summoned to take up the difficult task. But it proved too great for even his fighting energy. The party was divided. Gross corruption in the awarding of public contracts had been brought to light. The farmers were demanding a lower tariff. The leader of the Opposition was proving to have all the astuteness and the mastery of his party which had marked Macdonald and a courage in his convictions which promised well. Defeat seemed inevitable unless a new issue which had invaded federal politics, the Manitoba school question, should prove more dangerous to the Opposition than to the forces of the Government.

The Manitoba school question was an echo of the racial and religious strife which followed the execution of Riel and in which the Jesuits' Estates controversy was an episode. In the early days of the province, when it was still uncertain which religion would be dominant among the settlers, a system of state-aided denominational schools had been established. In 1890 the Manitoba Government swept this system away and replaced it by a single system of non-sectarian and state-supported schools which were practically the same as the old Protestant schools. Any Roman Catholic who did not wish to send his children to such a school was thus compelled to pay for the maintenance of a parochial school as well as to pay taxes for the public schools. A provision of the Confederation Act, inserted at the wish of the Protestant minority in Quebec, safeguarded the educational privileges of religious minorities. A somewhat similar clause had been inserted in the Manitoba Act of 1870. To this protection the Manitoba minority now appealed. The courts held that the province had the right to pass the law but also that the Dominion Government had the constitutional right to pass remedial legislation restoring in some measure the privileges taken away. The issue was thus forced into federal politics.

A curious situation then developed. The leader of the Government, Sir Mackenzie Bowell, was a prominent Orangeman. The leader of the Opposition, Wilfrid Laurier, was a Roman Catholic. The Government, after a vain attempt to induce the province to amend its measure, decided to pass a remedial act compelling it to restore to the Roman Catholics their rights. The policy of the Opposition leader was awaited with keen expectancy. Strong pressure was brought upon Laurier by the Roman Catholic hierarchy of Quebec. Most men expected a temporizing compromise. Yet the leader of the Opposition came out strongly and flatly against the Government's measure. He agreed that a wrong had been done but insisted that compulsion could not right it and promised that, if in power, he would follow the path of conciliation. At once all the wrath of the hierarchy was unloosed upon him, and all its influence was thrown to the support of the Government. Yet when the Liberals blocked the Remedial Bill by obstructing debate until the term of Parliament expired, and forced an election on this issue in the summer of 1896, Quebec gave a big majority to Laurier, while Manitoba stood behind the party which had tried to coerce it. The country over, the Liberals had gained a decisive majority. The day of new leaders and a new policy had dawned at last.

CHAPTER V

THE YEARS OF FULFILMENT

WILFRID LAURIER was summoned to form his first
Cabinet in July, 1896. For eighteen years previous
to that time the Liberals had sat in what one of
their number used to call "the cold shades of Opposition." For half of that term Laurier had been
leader of the party, confined to the negative task
of watching and criticizing the administration of
his great predecessor and of the four premiers who
followed in almost as many years. Now he was
called to constructive tasks. Fortune favored him
by bringing him to power at the very turn of the
tide; but he justified fortune's favor by so steering
the ship of state as to take full advantage of wind
and current. Through four Parliaments, through
fifteen years of office, through the time of fruition
of so many long-deferred hopes, he was to guide
the destinies of the nation.

Laurier began his work by calling to his Cabinet

not merely the party leaders in the federal arena but four of the outstanding provincial Liberals — Oliver Mowat, Premier of Ontario, William S. Fielding, Premier of Nova Scotia, Andrew G. Blair, Premier of New Brunswick, and, a few months later, Clifford Sifton of Manitoba. The Ministry was the strongest in individual capacity that the Dominion had yet possessed. The prestige of the provincial leaders, all men of long experience and tested shrewdness, strengthened the Administration in quarters where it otherwise would have been weak, for there had been many who doubted whether the untried Liberal party could provide capable administrators. There had also been many who doubted the expediency of making Prime Minister a French-Canadian Catholic. Such doubters were reassured by the presence of Mowat and Fielding, until the Prime Minister himself had proved the wisdom of the choice. There were others who admitted Laurier's personal charm and grace but doubted whether he had the political strength to control a party of conflicting elements and to govern a country where different race and diverging religious and sectional interests set men at odds. Here again time proved such fears to be groundless. Long before Laurier's long

term of office had ended, any distrust was transformed into the charge of his opponents that he
played the dictator. His courtly manners were
found not to hide weakness but to cover strength.

The first task of the new Government was to
settle the Manitoba school question. Negotiations
which were at once begun with the provincial
Government were doubtless made easier by the
fact that the same party was in power at Ottawa
and at Winnipeg, but it was not this fact alone
which brought agreement. The Laurier Government, unlike its predecessor, did not insist on the
restoration of separate schools. It accepted a
compromise which retained the single system of
public schools, but which provided religious teaching in the last half hour of school and, where numbers warranted, a teacher of the same faith as the
pupils. The compromise was violently denounced
by the Roman Catholic hierarchy but, except in
two cities, where parochial schools were set up, it
was accepted by the laity.

With this thorny question out of the way, the
Government turned to what it recognized as its
greatest task, the promotion of the country's
material prosperity. For years industry had been
at a standstill. Exports and imports had ceased

to expand; railway building had halted; emigrants
outnumbered immigrants. The West, the center
of so many hopes, the object of so many sacrifices,
had not proved the El Dorado so eagerly sought
by fortune hunters and home builders. There
were little over two hundred thousand white men
west of the Great Lakes. Homesteads had been
offered freely; but in 1896 only eighteen hundred
were taken up, and less than a third of these by
Canadians from the East. The stock of the Canadian Pacific was selling at fifty. All but a few had
begun to lose faith in the promise of the West.

Then suddenly a change came. The failure of
the West to lure pioneers was not due to poverty
of soil or lack of natural riches: its resources were
greater than the most reckless orator had dreamed.
It was merely that its time had not come and that
the men in charge of the country's affairs had not
thrown enough energy into the task of speeding
the coming of that time. Now fortune worked
with Canada, not against it. The long and steady
fall of prices, and particularly of the prices of farm
products, ended; and a rapid rise began to make
farming pay once more. The good free lands of the
United States had nearly all been taken up. Canada's West was now the last great reserve of

free and fertile land. Improvements in farming methods made it possible to cope with the peculiar problems of prairie husbandry. British capital, moreover, no longer found so ready an outlet in the United States, which was now financing its own development; and it had suffered severe losses in Argentine smashes and Australian droughts. Capital, therefore, was free to turn to Canada.

But it was not enough merely to have the resources; it was essential to display them and to disclose their value. Canada needed millions of men of the right stock, and fortunately there were millions who needed Canada. The work of the Government was to put the facts before these potential settlers. The new Minister of the Interior, Clifford Sifton, himself a western man, at once began an immigration campaign which has never been equaled in any country for vigor and practical efficiency. Canada had hitherto received few settlers direct from the Continent. Western Europe was now prosperous, and emigrants were few. But eastern Europe was in a ferment, and thousands were ready to swarm to new homes overseas. The activities of a subsidized immigration agency, the North Atlantic Trading Company, brought great numbers of these peoples. Foremost in numbers were the Ruthenians from Galicia. Most distinctive were the Doukhobors or Spirit Wrestlers of Southern Russia, about ten thousand of whom were brought to Canada at the instance of Tolstoy and some English Quakers to escape persecution for their refusal to undertake military service. The religious fanaticism of the Doukhobors, particularly when it took the form of midwinter pilgrimages in nature's garb, and the clannishness of the Ruthenians, who settled in solid blocks, gave rise to many problems of government and assimilation which taught Canadians the unwisdom of inviting immigration from eastern or southern Europe. Ruthenians and Poles, however, continued to come down to the eve of the Great War, and nearly all settled on western lands. Jewish Poland sent its thousands who settled in the larger cities, until Montreal had more Jews than Jerusalem and its Protestant schools held their Easter holidays in Passover. Italian navvies came also by the thousands, but mainly as birds of passage; and Greeks and men from the Balkan States were limited in numbers. Of the three million immigrants who came to Canada from the beginning of the century to the outbreak of the war, some eight hundred thousand came from

continental Europe, and of these the Ruthenians, Jews, Italians, and Scandinavians were the
most numerous.

It was in the United States that Canada made
the greatest efforts to obtain settlers and that she
achieved the most striking success. Beginning
in 1897 advertisements were placed in five or six
thousand American farm and weekly newspapers.
Booklets were distributed by the million. Hundreds of farmer delegates were given free trips
through the promised land. Agents were appointed in each likely State, with sub-agents who
were paid a bonus on every actual settler. The
first settlers sent back word of limitless land to be
had for a song, and of No. 1 Northern Wheat that
ran thirty or forty bushels to the acre. Soon immigration from the States began; the trickle became
a trek; the trek, a stampede. In 1896 the immigrants from the United States to Canada had been
so few as not to be recorded; in 1897 there were
2000; in 1899, 12,000; in the fiscal year 1902–03,
50,000; and in 1912–13, 139,000. The new immigrants proved to be the best of settlers; nearly
all were progressive farmers experienced in western
methods and possessed of capital. The counter-
movement from Canada to the United States never

wholly ceased, but it slackened and was much more than offset by this northward rush. Nothing so helped to confirm Canadian confidence in their own land and to make the outside world share this high estimate as this unimpeachable evidence from over a million American newcomers who found in Canada, between 1897 and 1914, greater opportunities than even the United States could offer. The Ministry then carried its propaganda to Great Britain. Newspapers, schools, exhibitions were used in ways which startled the stolid Englishman into attention. Circumstances played into the hands of the propagandists, who took advantage of the flow of United States settlers into the West, the Klondike gold fields rush, the presence of Laurier at the Jubilee festivities at London in 1897, Canada's share in the Boer War. British immigrants rose to 50,000 in 1903–04, to 120,000 in 1907–08, and to 150,000 in 1912–13. From 1897 to the outbreak of the war over 1,100,000 Britishers came to Canada. Three out of four were English, the rest mainly Scotch; the Irish, who once had come in tens of thousands and whose descendants still formed the largest element in the English-speaking peoples of Canada, now sent only one man for every twelve from England.

The gates of Canadian immigration, however, were not thrown open to all comers. The criminal, the insane and feeble-minded, the diseased, and others likely to become public charges, were barred altogether or allowed to remain provisionally, subject to deportation within three years. Immigrants sent out by British charitable societies were subjected, after 1908, to rigid inspection before leaving England. No immigrant was admitted without sufficient money in his purse to tide over the first few weeks, unless he were going to farm work or responsible relatives. Asiatics were restricted by special regulations. Steadily the bars were raised higher.

Not all the 3,000,000 who came to Canada between 1897 and 1914 remained. Many drifted across the border; many returned to their old homes, their dreams fulfilled or shattered; yet the vast majority remained. Never had any country so great a task of assimilation as faced Canada, with 3,000,000 pouring into a country of 5,000,000 in a dozen years. Fortunately the great bulk of the newcomers were of the old stocks.

Closely linked with immigration in promoting the prosperity of the country were the land policy and the railway policy of the Administration. The system of granting free homesteads to settlers was continued on an even more generous scale. The 1800 entries for homesteads in 1896 had become 40,000 ten years later. In 1906 land equal in area to Massachusetts and Delaware was given away; in 1908 a Wales, in 1909 five Prince Edward Islands, and in 1910 and 1911 a Belgium, a Netherlands, and two Montenegros passed from the state to the settler. Unfortunately not every homesteader became an active farmer, and production, though mounting fast, could not keep pace with speculation.

Railway building had almost ceased after the completion of the Canadian Pacific system. Now it revived on a greater scale than ever before. In the twenty years after 1896 the miles in operation grew from 16,000 to nearly 40,000. Two new trans-continentals were added, and the older roads took on a new lease of life. At the end of this period of expansion, only the United States, Germany, and Russia had railroad mileage exceeding that of Canada. Much of the building was premature or duplicated other roads. The scramble for state aid, federal and provincial, had demoralized Canadian politics. A large part of the notes the country rashly backed, by the policy of guaranteeing bond issues, were in time presented for payment. Yet the railway policies of the period were broadly justified. New country was opened to settlers; outlets to the sea were provided; capital was obtained in the years when it was still abundant and cheap; the whole industry of the country was stimulated; East was bound closer to West and depth was added to length.[1]

The opening of the West brought new prosperity to every corner of the East. Factories found growing markets; banks multiplied branches and business; exports mounted fast and imports faster; closer relations were formed with London and New York financial interests; mushroom millionaires, country clubs, city slums, suburban subdivisions, land booms, grafting aldermen, and all the apparatus of an advanced civilization grew apace. A new self-confidence became the dominant note alike of private business and of public policy.

With industrial prosperity, political unity became assured. Canada became more and more a name of which all her sons were proud. Expansion

[1] During the Great War it became necessary for the Federal Government to take over both the National Transcontinental, running from Moncton in New Brunswick to Winnipeg, and the Canadian Northern, running from ocean to ocean, and to incorporate both, along with the Intercolonial, in the Canadian National Railways, a system fourteen thousand miles in length.

brought men of the different provinces together. The Maritime Provinces first felt fully at one with the rest of Canada when Vancouver and Winnipeg rather than Boston and New York called their sons. Even Ontario and Quebec made some advance toward mutual understanding, though clerical leaders who sought safety for their Church in the isolation of its people, imperialists who drove a wedge between Canadians by emphasizing Anglo-Saxon racial ties, and politicians of the baser sort exploiting race prejudice for their own gain, opened rifts in a society already seamed by differences of language and creed. In the West unity was still harder to secure, for men of all countries and of none poured into a land still in the shaping. The divergent interests of the farming, free trade West and of the manufacturing, protectionist East made for friction. Fortunately strong ties held East and West together. Eastern Canadians or their sons filled most of the strategic posts in Government and business, in school and church and press in the West. Transcontinental railways, chartered banks with branches and interests in every province, political parties organizing their forces from coast to coast, played their part. Much had been accomplished; but much remained to be done.

With this background of rapid industrial development and growing national unity, Canada's relations with the Empire, with her sister democracy across the border, and with foreign states, took on new importance and divided interest with the changes in her internal affairs.

From being a state wherein the mother country exercised control and the colonies yielded obedience the Empire was rapidly being transformed into a free and equal partnership of independent commonwealths under one king. Out of the clash of rival theories and conflicting interests a new ideal and a new reality had developed. The policy of imperial coöperation — the policy whereby each great colony became independent of outside control but voluntarily acted in concert with the mother country and the sister states on matters of common concern — sought to reconcile liberty and unity, nationhood and empire, to unite what was most practicable in the aims of the advocates of independence and the advocates of imperial federation. The movement developed unevenly. At the outbreak of the Great War, it was still incomplete. The ideal was not always clearly or consciously held in the Empire itself and was wholly ignored or misunderstood in Europe and

even in the United States. Yet in twenty years'
space it had become dominant in practice and
theory and had built up a new type of political
organization, a virtual league of nations, fruitful
for the future ordering of the world.

The three fields in which this new policy was
worked out were trade, defense, and political organization. Canada had asserted her right to control her tariff and commercial treaty relations as
she pleased. Now she used this freedom to offer,
without asking any return in kind, tariff privileges
to the mother country. In the first budget brought
down by the Minister of Finance in the Laurier
Cabinet, William S. Fielding, a reduction, by in-
stalments, of twenty-five per cent in tariff duties
was offered to all countries with rates as low as
Canada's — that is, to the United Kingdom and
possibly to the Netherlands and New South Wales.
The reduction was meant both as a fulfilment of
the Liberal party's free trade pledges and as a
token of filial good will to Britain. It was soon
found that Belgium and Germany, by virtue of
their special treaty rights, would claim the same
privileges as Britain, and that all other countries
with most favored nation clauses could then demand the same rates. This might serve the free

trade aims of the Fielding tariff but would block
its imperial purpose. If this purpose was to be
achieved, these treaties must be denounced. To
effect this was one of the tasks Laurier undertook
in his first visit to England in 1897.

The Diamond Jubilee of Queen Victoria, cele-
brating the sixtieth anniversary of her reign, was
made the occasion for holding the third Colonial
Conference. It was attended by the Premiers of
all the colonies. Among them Wilfrid Laurier, or
Sir Wilfrid as he now became, stood easily pre-
eminent. In the Jubilee festivities, among the
crowds in London streets and the gatherings in
court and council, his picturesque and courtly
figure, his unmistakable note of distinction, his
silvery eloquence, and, not least, the fact that this
ruler of the greatest of England's colonies was
wholly of French blood, made him the lion of the
hour. In the Colonial Conference, presided over
by Joseph Chamberlain, the new Colonial Secretary, Laurier achieved his immediate purpose.
The British Government agreed to denounce the
Belgian and German treaties, now that the preference granted her came as a free gift and not as
part of a bargain which involved Britain's abandonment of free trade. The other Premiers agreed

to consider whether Canada's preferential tariff policy could be followed. Chamberlain in vain urged defense and political policies designed to centralize power in London. He praised the action of the Australian colonies in contributing money to the British navy but could get no promise of similar action from the others. He urged the need of setting up in London an imperial council, with power somewhat more than advisory and likely "to develop into something still greater," but for this scheme he elicited little support. After the Conference Sir Wilfrid visited France and in ringing speeches in Paris did much to pave the way for the good understanding which later developed into the *entente cordiale*.

The glitter and parade of the Jubilee festivities soon gave way to a sterner phase of empire. For years South Africa had been in ferment owing to the conflicting interests of narrow, fanatical, often corrupt Boer leaders, greedy Anglo-Jewish mining magnates, and British statesmen — Rhodes, Milner, Chamberlain — dominated by the imperial idea and eager for an "all-red" South Africa. Eventually an *impasse* was reached over the question of the rights and privileges of British subjects in the Transvaal Republic. On October 9, 1899,

President Krüger issued his fateful ultimatum and war began.

What would be Canada's attitude toward this imperial problem? She had never before taken part in an overseas war. Neither her own safety nor the safety of the mother country was considered to be at stake. Yet war had not been formally declared before a demand arose among Canadians that their country should take a hand in rescuing the victims of Boer tyranny. The Venezuela incident and the recent Jubilee ceremonies had fanned imperialist sentiment. The growing prosperity was increasing national pride and making many eager to abandon the attitude of colonial dependence in foreign affairs. The desire to emulate the United States, which had just won more or less glory in its little war with Spain, had its influence in some quarters. Belief in the justice of the British cause was practically universal, thanks to the skillful manipulation of the press by the war party in South Africa. Leading newspapers encouraged the campaign for participation. Parliament was not in session, and the Government hesitated to intervene, but the swelling tide of public opinion soon warranted immediate action. Three days after the declaration of war an order in council was passed providing for a contingent of one thousand men. Other infantry battalions, Mounted Rifles, and batteries of artillery were dispatched later. Lord Strathcona, formerly Donald Smith of the Canadian Pacific syndicate, by a deed recalling feudal days, provided the funds to send overseas the Strathcona Horse, roughriders from the Canadian West. In the last years of the war the South African Constabulary drew many recruits from Canada. All told, over seven thousand Canadians crossed half the world to share in the struggle on the South African veldt.

The Canadian forces held their own with any in the campaign. The first contingent fought under Lord Roberts in the campaign for the relief of Kimberley; and it was two charges by Canadian troops, charges that cost heavily in killed and wounded, that forced the surrender of General Cronje, brought to bay at Paardeberg. One Canadian battery shared in the honor of raising the siege of Mafeking, where Baden-Powell was besieged, and both contingents marched with Lord Roberts from Bloemfontein to Pretoria and fought hard and well at Doornkop and in many a skirmish. Perhaps the politic generosity of the British leaders and the patriotic bias of correspondents exaggerated the importance of the share of the Canadian troops in the whole campaign; but their courage, initiative, and endurance were tested and proved beyond all question. Paardeberg sent a thrill of pride and of sorrow through Canada.

The only province which stood aloof from whole-hearted participation in the war was Quebec. Many French Canadians had been growing nervous over the persistent campaign of the imperialists. They exhibited a certain unwillingness to take on responsibilities, perhaps a survival of the dependence which colonialism had bred, a dawning aspiration toward an independent place in the world's work, and a disposition to draw tighter racial and religious lines in order to offset the emphasis which imperialists placed on Anglo-Saxon ties. Now their sympathies went out to a people, like themselves an alien minority brought under British rule, and in this attitude they were strengthened by the almost unanimous verdict of the neutral world against British policy. Laurier tried to steer a middle course, but the attacks of ultra-imperialists in Ontario and of ultra-nationalists in Quebec, led henceforward by a brilliant and eloquent grandson of Papineau, Henri Bourassa, hampered him at every turn. The South African War gave a new unity to English-speaking Canada, but it widened the gap between the French and English sections.

The part which Australia and New Zealand, like Canada, had taken in the war gave new urgency to the question of imperial relations. English imperialists were convinced that the time was ripe for a great advance toward centralization, and they were eager to crystallize in permanent institutions the imperial sentiment called forth by the war. When, therefore, the fourth Colonial Conference was summoned to meet in London in 1902 on the occasion of the coronation of Edward VII, Chamberlain urged with all his force and keenness a wide programme of centralized action. "Very great expectations," he declared in his opening address, "have been formed as to the results which may accrue from our meeting." The expectations, however, were doomed to disappointment. He and those who shared his hopes had failed to recognize that the war had called forth a new national consciousness in the Dominions, as the self-governing colonies now came to be termed, even more than it had developed imperial sentiment. In the smaller colonies, New Zealand, Natal, Cape of Good Hope, the old attitude of colonial dependence survived in larger measure; but in Canada and in Australia, now federated into commonwealths, national feeling was uppermost.

Chamberlain brought forward once more his proposal for an imperial council, to be advisory at first and later to attain power to tax and legislate for the whole Empire, but he found no support. Instead, the Conference itself was made a more permanent instrument of imperial coöperation by a provision that it should meet at least every four years. The essential difference was that the Conference was merely a meeting of independent Governments on an equal footing, each claiming to be as much "His Majesty's Government" as any other, whereas the council which Chamberlain urged in vain would have been a new Government, supreme over all the Empire and dominated by the British representatives. Chamberlain then suggested more centralized means of defense, grants to the British navy, and the putting of a definite proportion of colonial militia at the disposal of the British War Office for overseas service. The Cape and Natal promised naval grants; Australia and New Zealand increased their contributions for the maintenance of a squadron in Pacific waters; but Canada held back. The smaller colonies were sympathetic to the militia proposal; but Canada and Australia rejected it on the grounds that it was "objectionable in principle, as derogating from the powers of self-government enjoyed by them, and would be calculated to impede the general improvement in training and organization of their defense forces." Chamberlain's additional proposal of free trade within the Empire and of a common tariff against all foreign countries found little support. That each part of the Empire should control its own tariff and that it should make what concessions it wished on British imports, either as a part of a reciprocal bargain or as a free gift, remained a fixed idea in the minds of the leaders of the Dominions. Throughout the sessions it was Laurier rather than Chamberlain who dominated the Conference.

Balked in his desire to effect political or military centralization, Chamberlain turned anew to the possibilities of trade alliance. His tariff reform campaign of 1903, which was a sequel to the Colonial Conference of 1902, proposed that Great Britain set up a tariff, incidentally to protect her own industries and to have matter for bargaining with foreign powers, but mainly in order to keep the colonies within her orbit by offering them special terms. In this way the Empire would become once more self-sufficient. The issue thus thrust upon Great Britain and the Empire in general was primarily a contest between free traders and protectionists, not between the supporters of coöperation and the supporters of centralization. On this basis the issue was fought out in Great Britain and resulted in the overwhelming victory of free trade and the Liberal party, aided as they were by the popular reaction against the jingoist policy which had culminated in the war. When the fifth Conference, now termed Imperial instead of Colonial, met in 1907, there was much impassioned advocacy of preference and protection on the part of Alfred Deakin of Australia and Sir L. S. Jameson of the Cape; but the British representatives stuck to their guns and, in Winston Churchill's phrase, the door remained "banged, barred, and bolted" against both policies. At this conference Laurier took the ground that, while Canada would be prepared to bargain preference for preference, the people of Great Britain must decide what fiscal system would best serve their own interests. A consistent advocate of home rule, he was willing, unlike some of his colleagues, from the other Dominions, to let the United Kingdom control its own affairs.

The defense issue had slumbered since the Boer War. Now the unbounded ambitions of Germany gave it startling urgency. It was about 1908 that the British public first became seriously alarmed over the danger involved in the lessening margin of superiority of the British over the German navy. The alarm was echoed throughout the Dominions. The Kaiser's challenge threatened the safety not only of the mother country but of every part of the Empire. Hitherto the Dominions had done little in the way of naval defense, though they had one by one assumed full responsibility for their land defense. The feeling had been growing that they should take a larger share of the common burden. Two factors, however, had blocked advance in this direction. The British Government had claimed and exercised full control of the issues of peace and war, and the Dominions were reluctant to assume responsibility for the consequences of a foreign policy which they could not direct. The hostility of the British Admiralty, on strategic and political grounds, to the plan of local Dominion navies, had prevented progress on the most feasible lines. The deadlock was a serious one. Now the imminence of danger compelled a solution. Taking the lead in this instance in the working out of the policy of colonial nationalism, Australia had already insisted upon abandoning the barren and inadequate policy of making a cash contribution for the support of a British squadron in Australasian waters and had established a local navy, manned, maintained, and controlled by the Commonwealth. Canada decided to follow her example. In March, 1909, the Canadian House of Commons unanimously adopted a resolution in favor of establishing a Canadian naval service to coöperate in close relation with the British navy. During the summer a special conference was held in London attended by ministers from all the Dominions. At this conference the Admiralty abandoned its old position; and it was agreed that Australia and Canada should establish local forces, cruisers, destroyers, and submarines, with auxiliary ships and naval bases.

When the Canadian Parliament met in 1910, Sir Wilfrid Laurier submitted a Naval Service Bill, providing for the establishment of local fleets, of which the smaller vessels were to be built in Canada. The ships were to be under the control of the Dominion Government, which might, in case of emergency, place them at the disposal of the British Admiralty. The bill was passed in March. In the autumn two cruisers, the *Rainbow* and the *Niobe*, were bought from Britain to serve as training ships. In the following spring a naval college was opened at Halifax, and tenders were called for the construction, in Canada, of five cruisers and six destroyers. In June, 1911, at the regular Imperial Conference of that year, an agreement was reached regarding the boundaries of the Australian and Canadian stations and uniformity of training and discipline.

Then came the reciprocity fight and the defeat of the Government. No tenders had been finally accepted, and the new Administration of Premier Borden was free to frame its own policy.

The naval issue had now become a party question. The policy of a Dominion navy, a policy which was the logical extension of the principles of colonial nationalism and imperial coöperation which had guided imperial development for many years, was attacked by ultra-imperialists in the English-speaking provinces as strategically unsound and as leading inevitably to separation from the Empire. It was also attacked by the Nationalists of Quebec, the ultra-colonialists or provincialists, as they might more truly be termed, under the vigorous leadership of Henri Bourassa, as yet another concession to imperialism and to militarism. In

November, 1910, by alarming the habitant by pictures of his sons being dragged away by naval press
gangs, the Nationalists succeeded in defeating the
Liberal candidate in a by-election in Drummond-
Arthabaska, at one time Laurier's own constit-
uency. In the general election which followed in
1911, the same issue cost the Liberals a score of
seats in Quebec.

When, therefore, the new Prime Minister, Sir
Robert Borden, faced the issue, he endeavored to
frame a policy which would suit both wings of his
following. In 1912 he proposed as an emergency
measure to appropriate a sum sufficient to build
three dreadnoughts for the British navy, subject
to recall if at any time the Canadian people decided
to use them as the nucleus of a Canadian fleet.
At the same time he undertook to submit to the
electorate his permanent naval policy, as soon as
it was determined. What that permanent policy
would be he was unwilling to say, but the Prime
Minister made clear his own leanings by insisting
that it would take half a century to form a Canadian navy, which at best would be a poor and weak
substitute for the organization the Empire already
possessed. The contribution to the British navy
satisfied the ultra-imperialists, while the promise

of a referendum and the call for money alone, and
not men, appealed to the Nationalist wing.   Under
the impetuous control of its new head, Winston
Churchill, the British Admiralty showed that it
had repented its brief conversion to the Dominion
navy policy, by preparing an elaborate memoran-
dum to support Borden's proposals, and also by
formulating plans for imperial flying squadrons
to be supplied by the Dominions, which made
clear its wish to continue the centralizing policy
permanently.   The Liberal Opposition vigorously
denounced the whole dreadnought programme, ad-
vocating instead two Canadian fleet units somewhat larger than at first contemplated.   Their
obstruction was overcome in the Commons by the
introduction of the closure, but the Liberal majority in the Senate, on the motion of Sir George
Ross, a former Premier of Ontario, threw out the
bill by insisting that it should not be passed before
being "submitted to the judgment of the country."
This challenge the Government did not accept.
Until the outbreak of the war no further steps
were taken either to arrange for contribution or
to establish a Canadian navy, though the naval
college at Halifax was continued, and the training
cruisers were maintained in a half-hearted way.

In the Imperial Conference of 1911, one more attempt was made to set up a central governing authority in London. Sir Joseph Ward, of New Zealand, acting as the mouthpiece of the imperial federationists, urged the establishment, first of an Imperial Council of State and later of an Imperial Parliament. His proposals met no support. "It is absolutely impracticable," was Laurier's verdict. "Any scheme of representation — no matter what you call it, parliament or council — of the overseas Dominions, must give them so very small a representation that it would be practically of no value," declared Premier Morris of Newfoundland. "It is not a practical scheme," Premier Fisher of Australia agreed; "our present system of responsible government has not broken down." "The creation of some body with centralized authority over the whole Empire," Premier Botha of South Africa cogently insisted, "would be a step entirely antagonistic to the policy of Great Britain which has been so successful in the past. . . . It is the policy of decentralization which has made the Empire — the power granted to its various peoples to govern themselves." Even Premier Asquith of the United Kingdom declared the proposals "fatal to the very fundamental conditions on which our empire has been built up and carried on."

Stronger than any logic was the presence of Louis Botha in the conferences of 1907 and 1911. On the former occasion it was only five years since he had been in arms against Great Britain. The courage and vision of Sir Henry Campbell-Bannerman in granting full and immediate self-government to the conquered Boer republics had been justified by the results. Once more freedom proved the only enduring basis of empire. Botha's task in attempting to make Boer and Briton work together, first in the Transvaal, and, after 1910, in the Union of South Africa, had not been an easy one. Attacked by extremists from both directions, he faced much the same difficulties as Laurier, and he found in Laurier's friendship, counsel, and example much that stood him in good stead in the days of stress to come.

Not less important than the relations with the United Kingdom in this period were the relations with the United States. The Venezuela episode was the turning point in the relations between the United States and the British Empire. Both in Washington and in London men had been astounded to find themselves on the verge of war. The danger passed, but the shock awoke thousands to a realization of all that the two peoples had in common and to the need of concerted effort to remove the sources of friction. Then hard on the heels of this episode followed the Spanish-American War.[1] Not the least of its by-products was a remarkable improvement in the relations of the English-speaking nations. The course of the war, the intrigues of European courts to secure intervention on behalf of Spain, and the lining up of a British squadron beside Dewey in Manila Bay when a German Admiral blustered, revealed Great Britain as the one trustworthy friend the United States possessed abroad. The annexation of the Philippines and the definite entry of the United States upon world politics broke down the irresponsible isolation which British ministers had found so much of a barrier to diplomatic accommodations. With John Hay and later Elihu Root at the State Department, and Lansdowne and Grey at the Foreign Office in London, there began an era of good feeling between the two countries.

Ottawa and Washington were somewhat slower in coming to terms. Many difficulties can arise

[1] See *The Path of Empire.*

along a three thousand mile border, and with a people so sure of themselves as the Americans were at this period and a people so sensitive to any infringements of their national rights as the Canadians were, petty differences often loomed large. The Laurier Government, therefore, proposed shortly after its accession to power in 1896 that an attempt should be made to clear away all outstanding issues and to effect a trade agreement. A Joint High Commission was constituted in 1898. The members from the United States were Senator Fairbanks, Senator Gray, Representative Nelson Dingley, General Foster, J. A. Kasson, and T. J. Coolidge of the State Department. Great Britain was represented by Lord Herschell, who acted as chairman, Newfoundland by Sir James Winter, and Canada by Sir Wilfrid Laurier, Sir Richard Cartwright, Sir Louis Davies, and John Charlton, M. P.

The Commission held prolonged sittings, first at Quebec and later at Washington, and reached tentative agreement on nearly all of the troublesome questions at issue. The bonding privileges on both sides the border were to be given an assured basis; the unneighborly alien labor laws were to be relaxed; the Rush-Bagot Convention regarding armament on the Great Lakes was to be revised; Canadian vessels were to abandon pelagic sealing in Bering Sea for a money compensation; and a reciprocity treaty covering natural products and some manufactures was sketched out. Yet no agreement followed. One issue, the Alaska boundary, proved insoluble, and as no agreement was acceptable which did not cover every difference, the Commission never again assembled after its adjournment in February, 1899.

The boundary between Alaska and the Dominion was the only bit of the border line not yet determined. As in former cases of boundary disputes, the inaccuracies of map makers, the ambiguities of diplomats, the clash of local interests, and stiff-necked national pride made a settlement difficult. In 1825 Russia and Great Britain had signed a treaty which granted Russia a long panhandle strip down the Pacific coast. With the purchase of Alaska in 1867 the United States succeeded to Russia's claim. With the growth of settlement in Canada this long barrier down half of her Pacific coast was found to be irksome. Attempt after attempt to have the line determined only added to the stock of memorials in official pigeonholes. Then came the discovery of gold in the Klondike in 1896, and the question of easy access by sea to the Canadian back country became an urgent one. Canada offered to compromise, admitting the American title to the chief ports on Lynn Canal, Dyea and Skagway, if Pyramid Harbor were held Canadian. She urged arbitration on the model the United States had dictated in the Venezuela dispute. But the United States was in possession of the most important points. Its people believed the Canadian claims had been trumped up when the Klondike fields were opened. The Puget Sound cities wanted no breach in their monopoly of the supply trade to the north. The only concession the United States would make was to refer the dispute to a commission of six, three from each country, with the proviso that no area settled by Americans should in any event pass into other hands. Canada felt that arbitration under these conditions would either end in deadlock, leaving the United States in possession, or in concession by one or more of the British representatives, and so declined to accept the proposed arrangement.

Finally, in 1903, agreement was reached between London and Washington to accept the tribunal proposed by the United States, which in turn withdrew its veto on the transfer of any settled area. Canada's reluctant consent was won by a provision that the members of the tribunal should be "impartial jurists of repute," sworn to render a judicial verdict. When Elihu Root, Senator Lodge, and Senator Turner were named as the American representatives, Ottawa protested that eminent and honorable as they were, their public attitude on this question made it impossible to consider them "impartial jurists." The Canadian Government in return nominated three judges, Lord Alverstone, Lord Chief Justice of England, Sir Louis Jetté, of Quebec, and Mr. Justice Armour, succeeded on his death by A. B. Aylesworth, a leader of the Ontario bar. The tribunal met in London, where the case was thoroughly argued.

The Treaty of 1825 had provided that the southern boundary should follow the Portland Canal to the fifty-sixth parallel of latitude and thence the summits of the mountains parallel to the coast, with the stipulation that if the summit of the mountains anywhere proved to be more than ten marine leagues from the ocean, a line drawn parallel to the windings of the coast not more than ten leagues distant should form the boundary. Three

questions arose: What was the Portland Canal?
Did the treaty assure Russia an unbroken strip
by making the boundary run round the ends of
deep inlets? Did mountains exist parallel to the
coast within ten leagues' distance? In October
these questions received their answer. Lord Alverstone and the three American members decided
in favor of the United States on the main issues.
The two Canadian representatives refused to
sign the award and denounced it as unjudicial
and unwarranted.

The decision set Canada aflame. Lord Alverstone was denounced in unmeasured terms. From
Atlantic to Pacific the charge was echoed that once
more the interests of Canada had been sacrificed
by Britain on the altar of Anglo-American friendship. The outburst was not understood abroad.
It was not, as United States opinion imagined,
merely childish petulance or the whining of a poor
loser. It was against Great Britain, not against
the United States, that the criticism was directed.
It was not the decision, but the way in which it
was made, that roused deep anger. The decision
on the main issue, that the line ran back of even
the deepest inlets and barred Canada from a single harbor, though unwelcome, was accepted as a

judicial verdict and has since been little questioned. The finding that the boundary should follow certain mountains behind those Canada urged, but short of the ten league line, was attacked by the Canadian representatives as a compromise, and its judicial character is certainly open to some doubt. But it was on the third finding that the thunders broke. The United States had contended that the Portland Channel of the treaty makers ran south of four islands which lay east of Prince of Wales Island, and Canada that it ran north of these islands. Lord Alverstone, after joining in a judgment with the Canadian commissioners that it ran north, suddenly, without any conference with them, and, as the wording of the award showed, by agreement with the United States representatives, announced that it ran where no one had ever suggested it could run, north of two and south of two, thus dividing the land in dispute. The islands were of little importance even strategically, but the incontrovertible evidence that instead of a judicial finding a political compromise had been effected was held of much importance. After a time the storm died down, but it revealed one unmistakable fact: Canadian nationalism was growing fully as fast as Canadian imperialism.

The relations between Canada and the United States now came to show the effect of increasingly close business connections. The northward trek of tens of thousands of American farmers was under way. United States capitalists began to invest heavily in farm and timber lands. Factory after factory opened a Canadian branch. Ten years later these investments exceeded six hundred millions. In the West, James J. Hill was planning the expansion of the Great Northern system throughout the prairie provinces and was securing an interest in the great Crow's Nest Pass coal fields. Tourist travel multiplied. The two peoples came to know each other better than ever before, and with knowledge many prejudices and misunderstandings vanished. Canada's growing prosperity did not merely bring greater individual intercourse; it made the United States as a whole less patronizing in its dealings with its neighbor and Canada less querulous and thin-skinned.

In this more favorable temper many old issues were cleared off the slate. The northeastern fisheries question, revived by a conflict between Newfoundland and the United States as to treaty privileges, was referred to the Hague Court in 1909. The verdict of the arbitrators recognized a measure of right in the contentions of both sides. A detailed settlement was prescribed which was accepted without demur in the United States, Newfoundland, and Canada alike. Pelagic sealing in the North Pacific was barred in 1911 by an international agreement between the United States, Great Britain, Japan, and Russia. Less success attended the attempt to arrange joint action to regulate and conserve the fisheries of the Great Lakes and the salmon fisheries of the Pacific, for the treaty drawn up in 1911 by the experts from both countries failed to pass the United States Senate.

But the most striking development of the decade was the businesslike and neighborly solution found for the settlement of the boundary waters controversy. The growing demands for the use of streams such as the Niagara, the St. Lawrence, and the Sault for power purposes, and of western border rivers for irrigation schemes, made it essential to take joint action to reconcile not merely the conflicting claims from the opposite sides of the border but the conflicting claims of power and navigation and other interests in each country. In 1905 a temporary waterways commission was appointed, and four years later the Boundary

Waters Treaty provided for the establishment of a permanent Joint High Commission, consisting of three representatives from each country, and with authority over all cases of use, obstruction, or diversion of border waters. Individual citizens of either country were allowed to present their case directly before the Commission, an innovation in international practice. Still more significant of the new spirit was the inclusion in this treaty of a clause providing for reference to the Commission, with the consent of the United States Senate and the Dominion Cabinet, of any matter whatever at issue between the two countries. With little discussion and as a matter of course, the two democracies, in the closing years of a full century of peace, thus made provision for the sane and friendly settlement of future line-fence disputes.

The chief barrier to good relations was the customs tariff. Protectionism, and the attitude of which it was born and which it bred in turn, was still firmly entrenched in both countries. Tariff bars, it is true, had not been able to prevent the rapid growth of trade; imports from the United States to Canada had grown especially fast and Canada now ranked third in the list of the Republic's customers. Yet in many ways the tariff hindered free intercourse. Though every dictate of self-interest and good sense demanded a reduction of duties, Canada would not and did not take the initiative. Time and again she had sought reciprocity, only to have her proposals rejected, often with contemptuous indifference. When Sir Wilfrid Laurier announced in 1900 that there would be no more pilgrimages to Washington, he voiced the almost unanimous opinion of a people whose pride had been hurt by repeated rebuffs.

Meanwhile protectionist sentiment had grown stronger in Canada. The opening of the West had given an expanding market for eastern factories and had seemingly justified the National Policy. The Liberals, the traditional upholders of freer trade, after some initial redemptions of their pledges, had compromised with the manufacturing interests. The Conservatives, still more protectionist in temper, voiced in Parliament little criticism of this policy, and the free trade elements among the farmers were as yet unorganized and inarticulate. Signs of this protectionist revival, which had in it, as in the seventies, an element of nationalism, were many. A four-story tariff was erected. The lowest rates were those granted the United Kingdom; then came the intermediate tariff, for the products of countries giving Canada special terms; next the general tariff; and, finally, the surtax for use against powers discriminating in any special degree against the Dominion. The provinces one by one forbade the export of pulp wood cut on Crown Lands, in order to assure its manufacture into wood pulp or paper in Canada. The Dominion in 1907 secured the abrogation of the postal convention made with the United States in 1875 providing for the reciprocal free distribution of second class mail matter originating in the other country. This step was taken at the instance of Canadian manufacturers, alarmed at the effect of the advertising pages of United States magazines in directing trade across the line. Yet even with such developments, the Canadian tariff remained lower than its neighbor's.

In the United States the tendency was in the other direction. With the growth of cities, the interests of the consumers of foods outweighed the influence of the producers. Manufacturers in many cases had reached the export stage, where foreign markets, cheap food, and cheap raw materials were more necessary than a protected home market. The "muckrakers" were at the height of their activity; and the tariff, as one instrument of

16

corruption and privilege, was suffering with the popular condemnation of all big interests. United States newspapers were eager for free wood pulp and cheaper paper, just as Canadian newspapers defended the policy of checking export. It was not surprising, therefore, that reciprocity with Canada, as one means of increasing trade and reducing the tariff, took on new popularity. New England was the chief seat of the movement, with Henry M. Whitney and Eugene N. Foss as its most persistent advocates. Detroit, Chicago, St. Paul, and other border cities were also active.

Official action soon followed this unofficial campaign. Curiously enough, it came as an unexpected by-product of a further experiment in protection, the Payne-Aldrich tariff. For the first time in the experience of the United States this tariff incorporated the principle of minimum and maximum schedules. The maximum rates, fixed at twenty-five per cent ad valorem above the normal or minimum rates, were to be enforced upon the goods of any country which had not, before March 10, 1910, satisfied the President that it did not discriminate against the products of the United States. One by one the various nations demonstrated this to President Taft's satisfaction or with wry faces made the readjustments necessary. At last Canada alone remained. The United States conceded that the preference to the United Kingdom did not constitute discrimination, but it insisted that it should enjoy the special rates recently extended to France by treaty. In Canada this demand was received with indignation. Its tariff rates were much lower than those which the United States imposed, and its purchases in that country were twice as great as its sales. The demand was based on a sudden and complete reversal of the traditional American interpretation of the most favored nation policy. The President admitted the force of Canada's contentions, but the law left him no option. Fortunately it did leave him free to decide as to the adequacy of any concessions, and thus agreement was made possible at the eleventh hour. At the President's suggestion a conference at Albany was arranged, and on the 30th of March a bargain was struck. Canada conceded to the United States its intermediate tariff rates on thirteen minor schedules — chinaware, nuts, prunes, and whatnot. These were accepted as equivalent to the special terms given France, and Canada was certified as being entitled to minimum rates. The United States had saved its face.

Then to complete the comedy, Canada immediately granted the same concessions to all other countries, that is, made the new rates part of the general tariff. The United States ended where it began, in receipt of no special concessions. The motions required had been gone through; phantom reductions had been made to meet a phantom discrimination.

This was only the beginning of attempts at accommodation. The threat of tariff war had called forth in the United States loud protests against any such reversion to economic barbarism. President Taft realized that he had antagonized the growing low-tariff sentiment of the country by his support of the Payne-Aldrich tariff and was eager to set himself right. A week before the March negotiations were concluded, a Democratic candidate had carried a strongly Republican congressional district in Massachusetts on a platform of reciprocity with Canada. The President, therefore, proposed a bold stroke. He made a sweeping offer of better trade relations. Negotiations were begun at Ottawa and concluded in Washington. In January, 1911, announcement was made that a broad agreement had been effected. Grain, fruit, and vegetables, dairy and most farm products, fish, hewn timber and sawn lumber, and several

minerals were put on the free list. A few manufactures were also made free, and the duties on
meats, flour, coal, agricultural implements, and
other products were substantially reduced. The
compact was to be carried out, not by treaty, but
by concurrent legislation. Canada was to extend
the same terms to the most favored nations by
treaty, and to all parts of the British Empire
by policy.

For fifty years the administrations of the two
countries had never been so nearly at one. More
difficulty was met with in the legislatures. In
Congress, farmers and fishermen, standpat Republicans and Progressives hostile to the Administration, waged war against the bargain. It was
only in a special session, and with the aid of Democratic votes and a Washington July sun, that the
opposition was overcome. In the Canadian Parliament, after some initial hesitation, the Conservatives attacked the proposal. The Government
had a safe majority, but the Opposition resorted to
obstruction; and late in July, Parliament was suddenly dissolved and the Government appealed to
the country.

When the bargain was first concluded, the Canadian Government had imagined it would meet

little opposition, for it was precisely the type of agreement that Government after Government, Conservative as well as Liberal, had sought in vain for over forty years. For a day or two that expectation was justified. Then the forces of opposition rallied, timid questioning gave way to violent denunciation, and at last agreement and Government alike were swept away in a flood of popular antagonism.

One reason for this result was that the verdict was given in a general election, not in a referendum. The fate of the Government was involved; its general record was brought up for review; party ambitions and passions were stirred to the utmost. Fifteen years of officeholding had meant the accumulation of many scandals, a slackening in administrative efficiency, and the cooling by official compromise of the ardent faith of the Liberalism of the earlier day. The Government had failed to bring in enough new blood. The Opposition fought with the desperation of fifteen years of fasting and was better served by its press.

Of the side issues introduced into the campaign, the most important were the naval policy in Quebec and the racial and religious issue in the English-speaking provinces. The Government had to face what Sir Wilfrid Laurier termed "the unholy alliance" of Roman Catholic Nationalists under Bourassa in Quebec and Protestant Imperialists in Ontario. In the French-speaking districts the Government was denounced for allowing Canada to be drawn into the vortex of militarism and imperialism and for sacrificing the interests of Roman Catholic schools in the West. On every hand the naval policy was attacked as inevitably bringing in its train conscription to fight European wars — a contention hotly denied by the Liberals. The Conservative campaign managers made a working arrangement with the Nationalists as to candidates and helped liberally in circulating Bourassa's newspaper, *Le Devoir.* On the back "concessions" of Ontario a quieter but no less effective campaign was carried on against the domination of Canadian politics by a French Roman Catholic province and a French Roman Catholic Prime Minister. In vain the Liberals appealed to national unity or started back fires in Ontario by insisting that a vote for Borden meant a vote for Bourassa. The Conservative-Nationalist alliance cost the Government many seats in Quebec and apparently did not frighten Ontario.

Reciprocity, however, was the principal issue

everywhere except in Quebec. Powerful forces were arrayed against it. Few manufactures had been put on the free list, but the argument that the reciprocity agreement was the thin edge of the wedge rallied the organized manufacturers in almost unbroken hostile array. The railways, fearful that western traffic would be diverted to United States roads, opposed the agreement vigorously under the leadership of the ex-American chairman of the board of directors of the Canadian Pacific, Sir William Van Horne, who made on this occasion one of his few public entries into politics. The banks, closely involved in the manufacturing and railway interests, threw their weight in the same direction. They were aided by the prevalence of protectionist sentiment in the eastern cities and industrial towns, which were at the same stage of development and in the same mood as the cities of the United States some decades earlier. The Liberal fifteen-year compromise with protection made it difficult in a seven weeks' campaign to revive a desire for freer trade. The prosperity of the country and the cry, "Let well enough alone," told powerfully against the bargain. Yet merely from the point of view of economic advantage, the popular verdict would probably have been in its favor. The United States market no longer loomed so large as it had in the eighties, but its value was undeniable. Farmer, fisherman, and miner stood to gain substantially by the lowering of the bars into the richest market in the world. Every farm paper in Canada and all the important farm organizations supported reciprocity. Its opponents, therefore, did not trust to a direct frontal attack. Their strategy was to divert attention from the economic advantages by raising the cry of political danger. The red herring of annexation was drawn across the trail, and many a farmer followed it to the polling booth.

From the outset, then, the opponents of reciprocity concentrated their attacks on its political perils. They denounced the reciprocity agreement as the forerunner of annexation, the deathblow to Canadian nationality and British connection. They prophesied that the trade and intercourse built up between the East and the West of Canada by years of sacrifice and striving would shrivel away, and that each section of the Dominion would become a mere appendage to the adjacent section of the United States. Where the treasure was, there would the heart be also. After some years of reciprocity, the channels of Canadian trade would be so changed that a sudden return to high protection on the part of the United States would disrupt industry and a mere threat of such a change would lead to a movement for complete union.

This prophecy was strengthened by apposite quotations showing the existing drift of opinion in the United States. President Taft's reference to the "light and imperceptible bond uniting the Dominion with the mother country" and his "parting of the ways" speech received sinister interpretations. Speaker Champ Clark's announcement that he was in favor of the agreement because he hoped "to see the day when the American flag will float over every square foot of the British North American possessions" was worth tens of thousands of votes. The anti-reciprocity press of Canada seized upon these utterances, magnified them, and sometimes, it was charged, inspired or invented them. Every American crossroads politician who found a useful peroration in a vision of the Stars and Stripes floating from Panama to the North Pole was represented as a statesman of national power voicing a universal sentiment. The action of the Hearst papers in sending pro-reciprocity editions into the border cities of Canada made many votes — but not for reciprocity.

The Canadian public proved that it was unable to suffer fools gladly. It was vain to argue that all men of weight in the United States had come to understand and to respect Canada's independent ambitions; that in any event it was not what the United States thought but what Canada thought that mattered; or that the Canadian farmer who sold a bushel of good wheat to a United States miller no more sold his loyalty with it than a Kipling selling a volume of verse or a Canadian financier selling a block of stock in the same market. The flag was waved, and the Canadian voter, mindful of former American slights and backed by newly arrived Englishmen admirably organized by the anti-reciprocity forces, turned against any "entangling alliance." The prosperity of the country made it safe to express resentment of the slights of half a century or fear of this too sudden friendliness.

The result of the elections, which were held on September 21, 1911, was the crushing defeat of the Liberal party. A Liberal majority of forty-four in a house of two hundred and twenty-one members was turned into a Conservative majority of forty-nine. Eight cabinet ministers went down to defeat. The Government had a slight majority in the Maritime Provinces and Quebec, and a large majority in the prairie West, but the overwhelming victory of the Opposition in Ontario, Manitoba, and British Columbia turned the day.

The appeal to loyalty revealed much that was worthy and much that was sordid in Canadian life. It was well that a sturdy national self-reliance should be developed and expressed in the face of American prophets of "manifest destiny," and that men should be ready to set ideals above pocket. It was unfortunate that in order to demonstrate a loyalty which might have been taken for granted economic advantage was sacrificed; and it was disturbing to note the ease with which big interests with unlimited funds for organizing, advertising, and newspaper campaigning, could pervert national sentiment to serve their own ends. Yet this was possibly a stage through which Canada, like every young nation, had to pass; and the gentle art of twisting the lion's tail had proved a model for the practice of plucking the eagle's feathers.

The growth of Canada brought her into closer touch with lands across the sea. Men, money, and merchandise came from East and West; and with their coming new problems faced the Government of the Dominion. With Europe they were trade questions to solve, and with Asia the more delicate issues arising out of oriental immigration.

In 1907 the Canadian Government had established an intermediate tariff, with rates halfway between the general and the British preferential tariffs, for the express purpose of bargaining with other powers. In that year an agreement based substantially on these intermediate rates was negotiated with France, though protectionist opposition in the French Senate prevented ratification until 1910. Similar reciprocal arrangements were concluded in 1910 with Belgium, the Netherlands, and Italy. The manner of the negotiation was as significant as the matter. In the case of France the treaty was negotiated in Paris by two Canadian ministers, W. S. Fielding and L. P. Brodeur, appointed plenipotentiaries of His Majesty for that purpose, with the British Ambassador associated in what Mr. Arthur Balfour termed a "purely technical" capacity. In the case of the other countries even this formal recognition of the old colonial status was abandoned. The agreement with Italy was negotiated in Canada between "the Royal Consul of Italy for Canada, representing the government of the Kingdom of Italy, and the Minister of Finance of Canada, representing His Excellency the Governor General acting in conjunction with the King's Privy Council for Canada." The conclusions in these later instances were embodied in conventions, rather than formal treaties.

With one country, however, tariff war reigned instead of treaty peace. In 1899 Germany subjected Canadian exports to her general or maximum tariff, because the Dominion refused to grant her the preferential rates reserved for members of the British Empire group of countries. After four years' deliberation Canada eventually retaliated by imposing on German goods a special surtax of thirty-three and one-third per cent. The trade of both countries suffered, but Germany's, being more specialized, much the more severely. After seven years' strife, Germany took the initiative in proposing a truce. In 1910 Canada agreed to admit German goods at the rates of the general — not the intermediate — tariff, while Germany in return waived her protest against the British preference and granted minimum rates on the most important Canadian exports.

Oriental immigration had been an issue in Canada ever since Chinese navvies had been imported in the early eighties to work on the government sections of the Canadian Pacific Railway. Mine owners, fruit farmers, and contractors were anxious that the supply should continue unchecked; but, as in the United States, the economic objections of the labor unions and the political objections of the advocates of a "White Canada" carried the day.

Chinese immigration had been restricted in 1885 by a head tax of $50 on all immigrants save officials, merchants, or scholars; in 1901 this tax was doubled; and in 1904 it was raised to $500. In each case the tax proved a barrier only for a year or two, when wages would rise sufficiently to warrant Orientals paying the higher toll to enter the Promised Land. Japanese immigrants did not come in large numbers until 1906, when the activities of employment companies brought seven thousand Japanese by way of Hawaii. Agitators from the Pacific States fanned the flames of opposition in British Columbia, and anti-Chinese and anti-Japanese riots broke out in Vancouver in 1907. The Dominion Government then grappled with the question. Japan's national sensitiveness and her position as an ally of Great Britain called for diplomatic handling. A member of the Dominion Cabinet, Rodolphe Lemieux, succeeded in 1907 in negotiating at Tokio an agreement by which Japan herself undertook to restrict the number of passports issued annually to emigrants to Canada.

The Hindu migration, which began in 1907, gave rise to a still more delicate situation. What did the British Empire mean, many a Hindu asked, if British subjects were to be barred from British lands? The only reply was that the British Government which still ruled India no longer ruled the Dominions, and that it was on the Dominions that the responsibility for the exclusion policy must rest. In 1909 Canada suggested that the Indian Government itself should limit emigration, but this policy did not meet with approval at the time. Failing in this measure, the Laurier Government fell back on a general clause in the Immigration Act prohibiting the entrance of immigrants except by direct passage from the country of origin and on a continuous ticket, a rule which effectually barred the Hindu because of the lack of any direct steamship line between India and Canada. An Order-in-Council further required that immigrants from all Asiatic countries must possess at least $200 on entering Canada. The Borden Government supplemented these restrictions by a special Order-in-Council in 1913 prohibiting the landing of artisans or unskilled laborers of any race at ports in British Columbia, ostensibly because of depression in the labor market. The leaders of the Hindu movement, with apparently some German assistance, determined to test these restrictions. In May, 1914, there arrived at Vancouver from Shanghai a Japanese ship carrying four hundred Sikhs from India. A few were admitted, as having been previously domiciled in Canada; the others, after careful inquiry, were refused admittance and ordered to be deported. Local police were driven away from the ship when attempting to enforce the order, and the Government ordered H. M. C. S. *Rainbow* to intervene. By a curious irony of history, the first occasion on which this first Canadian warship was called on to display force was in expelling from Canada the subjects of another part of the British Empire. Further trouble followed when the Sikhs reached Calcutta in September, 1914, for riots took place involving serious loss of life and later an abortive attempt at rebellion. Fortunately there were good prospects that the Indian Government would in future accept the proposal made by Canada in 1909. At the Imperial Conference of 1917, where representatives of India were present for the first time, it was agreed

17

to recommend the principle of reciprocity in the treatment of immigrants, India thus being free to save her pride by imposing on men from the Dominions the same restrictions the Dominions imposed on immigrants from India.

But all these dealings with lands across the sea paled into insignificance beside the task imposed on Canada by the Great War. In the sudden crisis the Dominion attained a place among the nations which the slower changes of peace time could scarcely have made possible in decades.

When the war party in Germany and Austria-Hungary plunged Europe into the struggle the world had long been fearing, there was not a moment's hesitation on the part of the people of Canada. It was not merely the circumstance that technically Canada was at war when Britain was at war that led Canadians to instant action. The degree of participation, if not the fact of war, was wholly a matter for the separate Dominions. It was the deep and abiding sympathy with the mother country whose very existence was to be at stake. Later, with the unfolding of Germany's full designs of world dominance and the repeated display of her callous and ruthless policies, Canada comprehended the magnitude of the danger threatening all the world and grimly set herself to help end the menace of militarism once for all.

On August 1, 1914, two days before Belgium was invaded, and three days before war between Britain and Germany had been declared, the Dominion Government cabled to London their firm assurance that the people of Canada would make every sacrifice necessary to secure the integrity and honor of the Empire and asked for suggestions as to the form aid should take. The financial and administrative measures the emergency demanded were carried out by Orders-in-Council in accordance with the scheme of defense which only a few months before had been drawn up in a *War Book*. Two weeks later, Parliament met in a special four-day session and without a dissenting voice voted the war credits the Government asked and conferred upon it special war powers of the widest scope. The country then set about providing men, money, and munitions of war.

The day after war was declared, recruiting was begun for an expeditionary force of 21,000 men. Half as many more poured into the camp at Valcartier near Quebec; and by the middle of October this first Canadian contingent, over 30,000 strong, the largest body of troops which had ever crossed the Atlantic, was already in England, where its training was to be completed. As the war went on and all previous forecasts of its duration and its scale were far outrun, these numbers were multiplied many times. By the summer of 1917 over 400,000 men had been enrolled for service, and over 340,000 had already gone overseas, aside from over 25,000 Allied reservists.

Naturally enough it was the young men of British birth who first responded in large numbers to the recruiting officer's appeal. A military background, vivid home memories, the enlistment of kinsmen or friends overseas, the frequent slightness of local ties, sent them forth in splendid and steady array. Then the call came home to the native-born, and particularly to Canadians of English speech. Few of them had dreamed of war, few had been trained even in militia musters; but in tens of thousands they volunteered. From French-speaking Canada the response was slower, in spite of the endeavors of the leaders of the Opposition as well as of the Government to encourage enlistment. In some measure this was only to be expected. Quebec was dominantly rural; its men married young, and the country parishes had little touch with the outside world. Its people had no racial sympathy with Britain and their connection with France had long been cut by the cessation of immigration from that country. Yet this is not the complete explanation of that aloofness which marked a great part of Quebec. Account must be taken also of the resentment caused by exaggerated versions of the treatment accorded the French-Canadian minority in the schools of Ontario and the West, and especially of the teaching of the Nationalists, led by Henri Bourassa, who opposed active Canadian participation in the war. Lack of tact on the part of the Government and reckless taunts from extremists in Ontario made the breach steadily wider. Yet there were many encouraging considerations. Another grandson of the leader of '37, Talbot Papineau, fell fighting bravely, and it was a French-Canadian battalion, *Les Vingt Deuxièmes*, which won the honors at Courcelette.

When the war first broke out, no one thought of any but voluntary methods of enlistment. As the magnitude of the task came home to men and the example of Great Britain had its influence, voices began to be raised in favor of compulsion. Sir Robert Borden, the Premier, and Sir Wilfrid Laurier

alike opposed the suggestion.   Early in 1917 the
adoption of conscription in the United States,
and the need of reënforcements for the Canadian
forces at the front led the Prime Minister, immediately after his return from the Imperial Conference in London, to bring down a measure for compulsory service.   He urged in behalf of this course
that the need for men was urgent beyond all question; that the voluntary system, wasteful and un-
fair at best, had ceased to bring more than six
or seven thousand men a month, chiefly for other
than infantry ranks; and that only by compulsion
could Quebec be brought to shoulder her fair share
and the slackers in all the provinces be made to
rise to the need.   It was contended, on the other
hand, that great as was the need for men, the need
for food, which Canada could best of all countries
supply, was greater still; that voluntary recruiting
had yielded over four hundred thousand men, pro-
portionately equivalent to six million from the
United States, and was slackening only because
the reservoir was nearly drained dry; and that
Quebec could be brought into line more effectively
by conciliation than by compulsion.

The issue of conscription brought to an end the
political truce which had been declared in August,

1914. The keener partisans on both sides had not long been able to abide on the heights of non-political patriotism which they had occupied in the first generous weeks of the war. But the public was weary of party cries and called for unity. Suggestions of a coalition were made at different times. but the party in power, new to the sweets of office, confident of its capacity, and backed by a strong majority, gave little heed to the demand. Now, however, the strong popular opposition offered to the announcement of conscription led the Prime Minister to propose to Sir Wilfrid Laurier a coalition Government on a conscription basis. Sir Wilfrid, while continuing to express his desire to coöperate in any way that would advance the common cause, declined to enter a coalition to carry out a programme decided upon without consultation and likely, in his view, to wreck national unity without securing any compensating increase in numbers beyond what a vigorous and sympathetic voluntary campaign could yet obtain.

For months negotiations continued within Parliament and without. The Military Service Act was passed in August, 1917, with the support of the majority of the English-speaking members of the Opposition. Then the Government, which had already secured the passage of an Act providing for taking the votes of the soldiers overseas, forced through under closure a measure depriving of the franchise all aliens of enemy birth or speech who had been admitted to citizenship since 1902, and giving a vote to every adult woman relative of a soldier on active service. Victory for the Government now appeared certain. Leading English-speaking Liberals, particularly from the West, convinced that conscription was necessary to keep Canada's forces up to the need, or that the War Times Election Act made opposition hopeless, decided to accept Sir Robert Borden's offer of seats in a coalition Cabinet.

In the election of December, 1917, in which passion and prejudice were stirred as never before in the history of Canada, the Unionist forces won by a sweeping majority. Ontario and the West were almost solidly behind the Government in the number of members elected, Quebec as solidly against it, and the Maritime Provinces nearly evenly divided. The soldiers' vote, contrary to Australian experience, was overwhelmingly for conscription. The Laurier Liberals polled more civilian votes in Ontario, Quebec, Alberta, and British Columbia, and in the Dominion as a whole, than the united Liberal party had received in the Reciprocity election of 1911. The increase in the Unionist popular vote was still greater, however, and gave the Government fifty-eight per cent of the popular vote and sixty-five per cent of the seats in the House. Confidence in the administrative capacity of the new Government, the belief that it would be more vigorous in carrying on the war, the desire to make Quebec do its share, the influence of the leaders of the Western Liberals and of the Grain Growers' Associations, wholesale promises of exemption to farmers, and the working of the new franchise law all had their part in the result. Eight months after the Military Service Act was passed, it had added only twenty thousand men to the nearly five hundred thousand volunteers; but steps were then taken to cancel exemptions and to simplify the machinery of administration. Some eighty thousand men were raised under conscription, but the war, so far as Canada was concerned, was fought and won by volunteers.

"The self-governing British colonies," wrote Bernhardi before the war, "have at their disposal a militia, which is sometimes only in process of formation. They can be completely ignored so far as concerns any European theater of war." This contemptuous forecast might have been justified had German expectations of a short war been fulfilled. Though large and increasing sums had in recent years been spent on the Canadian militia and on a small permanent force, the work of building up an army on the scale the war demanded had virtually to be begun from the foundation. It was pushed ahead with vigor, under the direction, for the first three years, of the Minister of Militia, General Sir Sam Hughes. Many mistakes were made. Complaints of waste in supply departments and of slackness of discipline among the troops were rife in the early months. But the work went on; and when the testing time came, Canada's civilian soldiers held their own with any veterans on either side the long line of trenches.

It was in April, 1915, at the second battle of Ypres — or, as it is more often termed in Canada, St. Julien or Langemarck — that the quality of the men of the first contingent was blazoned forth. The Germans had launched a determined attack on the junction of the French and Canadian forces, seeking to drive through to Calais. The use, for the first time, of asphyxiating gases drove back in confusion the French colonial troops on the left of the Canadians. Attacked and outflanked by a

German army of 150,000 men, four Canadian bri-
gades, immensely inferior in heavy artillery and tor-
tured by the poisonous fumes, filled the gap, hang-
ing on doggedly day and night until reënforcements
came and Calais was saved.   In sober retrospection
it was almost incredible that the thin khaki line had
held against the overwhelming odds which faced it.
A few weeks later, at Givenchy and Festubert, in the
same bloody salient of Ypres, the Canadian division
displayed equal courage with hardly equal success.
In the spring of 1916, when the Canadian forces
grew first to three and then to four divisions, heavy
toll was taken at St. Eloi and Sanctuary Wood.

When they were shifted from the Ypres sector
to the Somme, the dashing success at Courcelette
showed them as efficient in offense as in defense.
In 1917 a Canadian general, Sir Arthur Currie, three
years before only a business man of Vancouver,
took command of the Canadian troops.   The capture of Vimy Ridge, key to the whole Arras position, after months of careful preparation, the hard-
fought struggle for Lens, and toward the close of
the year the winning of the Passchendaele Ridge,
at heavy cost, were instances of the increasing
scale and importance of the operations entrusted
to Currie's men.

In the closing year of the war the Canadian corps played a still more distinctive and essential part. During the early months of 1918, when the Germans were making their desperate thrusts for Paris and the Channel, the Canadians held little of the line that was attacked. Their divisions had been withdrawn in turn for special training in open warfare movements, in close coöperation with tanks and air forces. When the time came to launch the Allied offensive, they were ready. It was Canadian troops who broke the hitherto unbreakable Wotan line, or Drocourt-Queant switch; it was Canadians who served as the spearhead in the decisive thrust against Cambrai; and it was Canadians who captured Mons, the last German stronghold taken before the armistice was signed, and thus ended the war at the very spot where the British "Old Contemptibles" had begun their dogged fight four years before.

Through all the years of war the Canadian forces never lost a gun nor retired from a position they had consolidated. Canadians were the first to practice trench raiding; and Canadian cadets thronged that branch of the service, the Royal Flying Corps, where steady nerves and individual initiative were at a premium. In countless actions they proved their fitness to stand shoulder to shoulder with the best that Britain and France and the United States could send: they asked no more than that. The casualty list of 220,000 men, of whom 60,000 sleep forever in the fields of France and Flanders and in the plains of England, witnesses the price this people of eight millions paid as its share in the task of freeing the world from tyranny.

The realization that in a world war not merely the men in the trenches but the whole nation could and must be counted as part of the fighting force was slow in coming in Canada as in other democratic and unwarlike lands. Slowly the industry of the country was adjusted to a war basis. When the conflict broke out, the country was pulling itself together after the sudden collapse of the speculative boom of the preceding decade. For a time men were content to hold their organization together and to avert the slackening of trade and the spread of unemployment which they feared. Then, as the industrial needs and opportunities of the war became clear, they rallied. Field and factory vied in expansion, and the Canadian contribution of food and munitions provided a very substantial share of the Allies' needs. Exports increased threefold, and the total trade was more than doubled as compared with the largest year before the war.

The financing of the war and of the industrial expansion which accompanied it was a heavy task. For years Canada had looked to Great Britain for a large share alike of public and of private borrowings. Now it became necessary not merely to find at home all the capital required for ordinary development but to meet the burden of war expenditure, and later to advance to Great Britain the funds she required for her purchase of supplies in Canada. The task was made easier by the effective working of a banking system which had many times proved its soundness and its flexibility. When the money market of Britain was no longer open to overseas borrowers, the Dominion first turned to the United States, where several federal and provincial loans were floated, and later to her own resources. Domestic loans were issued on an increasing scale and with increasing success, and the Victory Loan of 1918 enrolled one out of every eight Canadians among its subscribers. Taxation reached an adequate basis more slowly. Inertia and the influence of business interests led the Government to cling for the first two years to customs and excise duties as its main reliance. Then excess profits and income taxes of steadily increasing weight were imposed, and the burdens were distributed more fairly. The Dominion was able not only to meet the whole expenditure of its armed forces but to reverse the relations which existed before the war and to become, as far as current liabilities went, a creditor rather than a debtor of the United Kingdom.

It was not merely the financial relations of Canada with the United Kingdom which required readjustment. The service and the sacrifices which the Dominions had made in the common cause rendered it imperative that the political relations between the different parts of the Empire should be put on a more definite and equal basis. The feeling was widespread that the last remnants of the old colonial subordination must be removed and that the control exercised by the Dominions should be extended over the whole field of foreign affairs.

The Imperial Conference met in London in the spring of 1917. At special War Cabinet meetings the representatives of the Dominions discussed war plans and peace terms with the leaders of Britain. It was decided to hold a Conference immediately after the end of the war to discuss the future constitutional organization of the Empire. Premier

Borden and General Smuts both came out strongly against the projects of imperial parliamentary federation which aggressive organizations in Britain and in some of the Dominions had been urging. The Conference of 1917 recorded its view that any coming readjustment must be based on a full recognition of the Dominions as autonomous nations of an imperial commonwealth; that it should recognize the right of the Dominions and of India to an adequate voice in foreign policy; and that it should provide effective arrangements for continuous consultation in all important matters of common concern and for such concerted action as the several Governments should determine. The policy of alliance, of coöperation between the Governments of the equal and independent states of the Empire, searchingly tested and amply justified by the war, had compelled assent.

The coming of peace gave occasion for a wider and more formal recognition of the new international status of the Dominions. It had first been proposed that the British Empire should appear as a unit, with the representatives of the Dominions present merely in an advisory capacity or participating in turn as members of the British delegation. The Dominion statesmen assembled in London and Paris declined to assent to this proposal, and insisted upon representation in the Peace Conference and in the League of Nations in their own right. The British Government, after some debate, acceded, and, with more difficulty, the consent of the leading Allies was won. The representatives of the Dominions signed the treaty with Germany on behalf of their respective countries, and each Dominion, with India, was made a member of the League. At the same time only the British Empire, and not any of the Dominions, was given a place in the real organ of power, the Executive Council of the League, and in many respects the exact relationship between the United Kingdom and the other parts of the Empire in international affairs was left ambiguous, for later events and counsel to determine. Many French and American observers who had not kept in close touch with the growth of national consciousness within the British Empire were apprehensive lest this plan should prove a deep-laid scheme for multiplying British influence in the Conference and the League. Some misunderstanding was natural in view not only of the unprecedented character of the Empire's development and polity, but of the incomplete and ambiguous nature of the compromise effected at Paris between the nationalist and the imperialist tendencies within the Empire. Yet the reluctance of the British imperialists of the straiter sect to accede to the new arrangement, and the independence of action of the Dominion representatives at the Conference, as in the stand of Premier Hughes of Australia on the Japanese demand for recognition of racial equality and in the statement of protest by General Smuts of South Africa on signing the treaty, made it clear that the Dominions would not be merely echoes. Borden and Botha and Smuts, though new to the ways of diplomacy, proved that in clear understanding of the broader issues and in moderation of policy and temper they could bear comparison with any of the leaders of the older nations.

The war also brought changes in the relations between Canada and her great neighbor. For a time there was danger that it would erect a barrier of differing ideals and contrary experience. When month after month went by with the United States still clinging to its policy of neutrality, while long lists of wounded and dead and missing were filling Canadian newspapers, a quiet but deep resentment, not without a touch of conscious superiority, developed in many quarters in the Dominion. Yet there were others who realized how difficult and how necessary it was for the United States to attain complete unity of purpose before entering the war, and how different its position was from that of Canada, where the political tie with Britain had brought immediate action more instinctive than reasoned. It was remembered, too, that in the first 360,000 Canadians who went overseas, there were 12,000 men of American birth, including both residents in Canada and men who had crossed the border to enlist. When the patience of the United States was at last exhausted and it took its place in the ranks of the nations fighting for freedom, the joy of Canadians was unbounded. The entrance of the United States into the war assured not only the triumph of democracy in Europe but the continuance and extension of frank and friendly relations between the democracies of North America. As the war went on and Canada and the United States were led more and more to pool their united resources, to coöperate in finance and in the supply of coal, iron, steel, wheat, and other war essentials, countless new strands were woven into the bond that held the two countries together. Nor was it material unity alone that was attained; in the utterances of the head of the Republic the highest aspirations of Canadians for the future ordering of the world found incomparable expression.

Canada had done what she could to assure the triumph of right in the war. Not less did she believe that she had a contribution to make toward that new ordering of the world after the war which alone could compensate her for the blood and treasure she had spent. It would be her mission to bind together in friendship and common aspirations the two larger English-speaking states, with one of which she was linked by history and with the other by geography. To the world in general Canada had to offer that achievement of difference in unity, that reconciliation of liberty with peace and order, which the British Empire was struggling to attain along paths in which the Dominion had been the chief pioneer. "In the British Commonwealth of Nations," declared General Smuts, "this transition from the old legalistic idea of political sovereignty based on force to the new social idea of constitutional freedom based on consent, has been gradually evolving for more than a century. And the elements of the future world government, which will no longer rest on the imperial ideas adopted from the Roman law, are already in operation in our Commonwealth of Nations and will rapidly develop in the near future." This may seem an idealistic aim; yet, as Canada's Prime Minister asked a New York audience in 1916, "What great and enduring achievement has the world ever accomplished that was not based on idealism?"

BIBLIOGRAPHICAL NOTE

For the whole period since 1760 the most comprehensive and thorough work is *Canada and its Provinces*, edited by A. Shortt and A. G. Doughty, 23 vols. (1914). W. Kingsford's *History of Canada*, 10 vols. (1887–1898), is badly written but is an ample storehouse of material. The *Chronicles of Canada* series (1914–1916) covers the whole field in a number of popular volumes, of which several are listed below. F. X. Garneau's *Histoire du Canada* (1845–1848; new edition, edited by Hector Garneau, 1913–), the classical French-Canadian record of the development of Canada down to 1840, is able and moderate in tone, though considered by some critics not sufficiently appreciative of the Church.

Of brief surveys of Canada's history the best are W. L. Grant's *History of Canada* (1914) and H. E. Egerton's *Canada* (1908).

The primary sources are abundant. The Dominion Archives have made a remarkable collection of original official and private papers and of transcripts of documents from London and Paris. See D. W. Parker, *A Guide to the Documents in the Manuscript Room at the Public Archives of Canada* (1914). Many of these documents are calendared in the *Report on Canadian Archives* (1882 to date), and complete reprints, systematically arranged and competently annotated, are being issued by the Archives Branch, of which A. Shortt and A. G. Doughty, *Documents Relating to the Constitutional History of Canada, 1759–1791*, and Doughty and McArthur, *Documents Relating to the Constitutional History of Canada, 1791–1818*, have already appeared. A useful collection of speeches and dispatches is found in H. E. Egerton and W. L. Grant, *Canadian Constitutional Development* (1907), and W. P. M. Kennedy has edited a somewhat larger collection, *Documents of the Canadian Constitution, 1759–1915* (1918). The later Sessional Papers and Hansards or Parliamentary Debates are easily accessible. Files of the older newspapers, such as the Halifax *Chronicle* (1820 to date, with changes of title), Montreal *Gazette* (1778 to date), Toronto *Globe* (1844 to date), *Manitoba Free Press* (1872 to date), Victoria *Colonist* (1858 to date), are invaluable. *The Dominion Annual Register and Review*, ed. by H. J. Morgan, 8 vols. (1879–1887) and *The Canadian Annual Review of Public Affairs*, by John Castell Hopkins (1901 to date), are useful for the periods covered.

For the first chapter, Sir Charles P. Lucas, *A History of Canada, 1763–1812* (1909) and A. G. Bradley, *The Making of Canada* (1908) are the best single volumes. William Wood, *The Father of British Canada* (*Chronicles of Canada*, 1916), records Carleton's defense of Canada in the Revolutionary War; and Justin H. Smith's *Our Struggle for the Fourteenth Colony* (1907) is a scholarly and detailed account of the same period from an American standpoint. Victor Coffin's *The Province of Quebec and the Early American Revolution* (1896), with a review of the same by Adam Shortt in the *Review of Historical Publications Relating to Canada*, vol. I (University of Toronto, 1897), and C. W. Alvord's *The Mississippi*

Valley in British Politics, 2 vols. (1917) should be consulted for an interpretation of the Quebec Act. For the general reader, W. S. Wallace's *The United Empire Loyalists* (*Chronicles of Canada*, 1914) supersedes the earlier Canadian compilations; C. H. Van Tyne's *The Loyalists in the American Revolution* (1902) and A. C. Flick's *Loyalism in New York during the American Revolution* (1901) embody careful researches by two American scholars. The War of 1812 is most competently treated by William Wood in *The War with the United States* (*Chronicles of Canada*, 1915); the naval aspects are sketched in Theodore Roosevelt's *The Naval War of 1812* (1882) and analyzed scientifically in A. T. Mahan's *Sea Power in its Relations to the War of 1812* (1905).

For the period, 1815–1841, W. S. Wallace's *The Family Compact* (*Chronicles of Canada*, 1915) and A. D. De Celles's *The Patriotes of '37* (*Chronicles of Canada*, 1916) are the most concise summaries. J. C. Dent's *The Story of the Upper Canadian Rebellion* (1885) is biased but careful and readable. *William Lyon Mackenzie*, by Charles Lindsey, revised by G. G. S. Lindsey (1908), is a sober defense of Mackenzie by his son-in-law and grandson. Robert Christie's *A History of the Late Province of Lower Canada*, 6 vols. (1848–1866) preserves much contemporary material. There are few secondary books taking the anti-popular side: T. C. Haliburton's *The Bubbles of Canada* (1839) records Sam Slick's opposition to reform; C. W. Robinson's *Life of Sir John Beverley Robinson* (1904) is a lifeless record of the greatest Compact leader. Lord Durham's *Report on the Affairs of British North America* (1839; available in Methuen reprint, 1902, or with introduction and notes by Sir Charles Lucas, 3 vols., 1912) is indispensable.

For the Union period there are several political biographies available. G. M. Wrong's *The Earl of Elgin* (1905), John Lewis's *George Brown* (1906), W. L. Grant's *The Tribune of Nova Scotia* (*Chronicles of Canada*, 1915), J. Pope's *Memoirs of the Right Honourable Sir John Alexander Macdonald*, 2 vols. (1894), J. Boyd's *Sir George Etienne Cartier* (1914), and O. D. Skelton's *Life and Times of Sir A. T. Galt* (1919), cover the political developments from various angles. A. H. U. Colquhoun's *The Fathers of Confederation* (*Chronicles of Canada*, 1916) is a clear and impartial account of the achievement of Confederation; while M. O. Hammond's *Canadian Confederation and its Leaders* (1917) records the service of each of its chief architects.

For the years since Confederation biographies again give the most accessible record. Sir John S. Willison's *Sir Wilfrid Laurier and the Liberal Party* (1903) is the best political biography yet written in Canada. Sir Richard Cartwright's *Reminiscences* (1912) reflects that statesman's individual and pungent views of affairs, while Sir Charles Tupper's *Recollections of Sixty Years* (1914) and John Castell Hopkins's *Life and Work of Sir John Thompson* (1895) give a Conservative version of the period. Sir Joseph Pope's *The Day of Sir John Macdonald* (*Chronicles of Canada*, 1915), and O. D. Skelton's *The Day of Sir Wilfrid Laurier* (*Chronicles of Canada*, 1916) between them cover the whole period briefly. L. J. Burpee's *Sandford Fleming* (1915) is one of the few biographies dealing with industrial as distinct from political leaders. Imperial relations may be studied in G. R. Parkin's *Imperial Federation, the Problem of National Unity* (1892) and in L. Curtis's *The Problem of the Commonwealth* (1916), which advocate imperial federation, and in R. Jebb's *The Britannic Question; a Survey of Alternatives* (1913), J. S. Ewart's *The Kingdom Papers* (1912–), and A. B. Keith's *Imperial Unity and the Dominions* (1916), which criticize that solution from different standpoints. The *Reports* of the Imperial Conferences of 1887, 1894, 1897, 1902, 1907, 1911, 1917, are of much value. Relations with the United States are discussed judiciously in W. A. Dunning's *The British Empire and the United States* (1914). Phases of Canada's recent development other than political are covered best in the volumes of *Canada and its Provinces*, a History of the Canadian people and their institutions, edited by A. Shortt and A. G. Doughty.

A useful guide to recent books dealing with Canadian history will be found in the annual *Review of Historical Publications Relating to Canada*, published by the University of Toronto (1896 to date).

INDEX